A Pr(

To My Friend Donna

Brenda Rogers

A

Promise Broken

The Book Series

Of

"The Damage of Deception"

Book One "The Damage of Deception"

Book Two "Empty Vows"

Book Three "A Unknown Love"

Book Four "A Promise Broken"

"He healeth the broken in heart, and bindeth up their wounds." Psalms147:3

Chapter One

I have never liked this long drive back home, after visiting with my mom.

Even though I enjoyed our visit, it was hard to say good bye and go back to my empty apartment, I had to keep reminding myself that it was my idea to move so far away from my family.

After college I was hoping to get a teaching position in my home town.

But after a year I accepted a fourth grade teaching position in Chicago, My mother tried to talk me out of going, but she knew how much I wanted to teach school.

This wasn't in my plans to live so far away, but my plans just didn't work out, because if they would have I would be married to my prince charming, living in a tri- level house down the street from my mother with two kids right now.

I knew how much my mom worried about me living alone in a big city, I wasn't happy about that part either.

Even though sometimes it gets lonely here, I was glad to come back to my little apartment, and my job and all my school children.

I love teaching fourth grade the age group was not to young that I had to constantly keep an eye on them and not to old where I had to also constantly keep an eye on them for different reasons.

But this age was fun and so far my students were Eagar to learn

I let them help me teach and always got all of them involved.

But after school and on weekends it could get really lonely I had friends at school and at my church but mostly single young couples and the couples my age were married and had families.

I dated a few times but nothing really serious, I wanted a family but as for now I was just going to have to be content just teaching my children, and sometimes I was content and then there was those lonely nights, when all my contentment went away.

There were times, I would decide to just go back home and wait until I could get a job closer to home.

Until the day Jeff Smith transferred to our school, to teach sixth grade.

My plans of going home were put on the back burner.

At first I thought he was very conceited and the other female teachers acted like school girls themselves whenever he was around, I kept my distant, he was very handsome, and he knew it.

I avoided Mr. Smith as much as I could but considering we both worked at the same school it was hard.

I started having lunch in my class room instead of going to the teacher's lounge.

When we would pass in the hall he always smiled at me with his beautiful straight white teeth and it would make my knees go weak.

The only conversation we ever had was about school.

It was on a Friday afternoon and I was grading papers at my desk when Jeff stuck his head in the door

"Hey Dana, you got a minute?" thinking he wanted to ask a question about school as he had before, I said of course.

But what he said next, took me by total surprise.

"I wanted to know if you would have dinner with me tonight, if you are not busy that is"

"Thank you for asking but I don't think that would be a good idea"

"Dana, I know you are a Christian, and I just want you to know that I respect that and would never ask you to go alone, it just so happens that a few other teachers with their husbands will be joining us, and you would be doing me a favor.

I don't know anyone in this town yet and wouldn't you hate for me to have to go alone?'

"Well I certainly wouldn't want that" I joked.

"Oh okay I guess I could, I don't have plans.

"My words were stumbling all over the place, and telling by his laughter it showed.

"I'm sorry didn't mean to startle you," he said.

"But thank you for doing this favor for me, you are kind."

"You are welcome, I would hate for you to be the fifth wheel, and I have never had dinner with my coworkers."

"Terrific "there's a nice Italian restaurant right down the street, everyone said they would like to try, if you like Italian?""

"I love Italian"

"Great, I will pick you up at six."

"I can meet you there at six O'clock."

"Prefect I will see you there " and he walked out of my room."

Immediately I got butterflies in my stomach.

Which was silly, I had been on a date before, just not in a while, and certainly not with someone as good looking as Jeff.

But anyway, this was not a date, just having dinner with some coworkers.

I had to keep reminding myself.

I carefully chose what to wear, getting mad at myself for acting like a silly school girl myself.

Jeff was new in town, he didn't know anyone and all the other female teachers at our school were too old or they were married, that is the only reason he ask me.

He said so himself. Just doing a favor for a coworker.

So the sooner I accepted that the better.

I just threw on a jean skirt and top, and walked out the door.

I needed to stop for gas but because it was almost six.

I decided to stop on my way home. I couldn't believe how nervous I was it was just dinner with a coworker.

Everyone was already there when I got to the restaurant.

And even though their husbands were seated right next to them, the woman still flirted. I was embarrassed for them, they acted so foolish.

But I was impressed with Jeff for not paying any attention to them,

The truth was I seemed to have all of his attention.

Jeff was easy to talk to, he joked around a lot which put me at ease, we talked about school and our students, it was really nice, and afterwards he walked me to my car.

"Thanks Dana for having supper with me tonight, it gets lonesome when you don't know anyone in a new town, I really enjoyed this."

"Yes so did I.

And I can remember when I got this job here, moving to a new town can be hard at first, but hey if you ever get lonely on a Sunday or Wednesday I attend a terrific church.

You are always welcome. I'm sure you would love it and it would give you the chance to meet people from here..."

"I would like that, where do you go to church at?"

I reached into my purse and took out a church card and handed it to him, the times and days we have church are on the card and the address, so please try to come."

"I will, thank you for inviting me, I will see you at school tomorrow, have a good night."

"Thank you, good night Jeff."

On the drive home I felt good that I had accepted his dinner invitation, because it gave me the opportunity to invite him to my church and to get to know the real Jeff, he was a very sweet guy that hid behind his joking and flirtation ways with the female teachers.

After stopping for gas I headed home with Jeff on my mind, This was good and if nothing comes of it, at lease I invited him to church, I kept telling myself but deep down I knew I wanted Jeff to like me.

"To him be glory and dominion for ever and ever. Amen." 1 Peter 5:11

Chapter two

I Have never liked pulling into the parking garage after dark it always gave me a strange feeling, I couldn't understand why they didn't have better lighting in here.

I quickly got out of my car and walked very fast out to the sidewall that led to my apartment, but before I reached the outside, I felt the blow that knocked me to the ground.

It came so fast I couldn't even react, I was being pulled to a dark corner of the garage he had his gloved hand over my mouth, and I couldn't breathe.

I knew I was going to die in my mind I just kept saying Jesus, Jesus.

He never took his hand away from my mouth it was so dark all I could see was an outline of my attacker.

Then he jumped off of me and ran, I just laid there I couldn't move, I was in so much pain and I was gasping for air.

Was this how I was going to die? I thought what if he comes back? I have to get out of here, so I crawled out of the dark corner then I got to my feet and I ran as fast as my legs would allow, out on the sidewall and I just started screaming I remember seeing a man and woman walking their dogs they came running to me.

"Are you okay?" the lady asked me.

"I was attacked in the parking garage just now"

"Oh you poor dear, Pete call 911" she told the man.

I got up and the lady took me to her apartment to wait for the police.

She gave me a wet cloth, but the man took it before I had a chance to get it.

"No wait for the police to get here, he told her.

When the police arrived I told them everything that had happened, after finding my purse that was still in the parking garage they took me to the hospital where again I was asked the same questions.

The woman police officer took pictures of my bruises and the cuts and scrapes on my knees, where he had dragged me.

I felt so dirty, I just wanted to go home and take a shower.

But at the same time I was so scared, what if he came back? What if he knew What Apartment I lived in?

I just started to cry.

"Honey is there any one you want to call," the lady police officer asked.

"Yes I want to call my mom" so she handed me my purse, where my cell phone was at.

I just told my mom that I had been attacked in my parking garage but I was okay.

I didn't want to scare her too badly.

My mother said she would be here in five hours but in the mean time she was calling my pastor to have them stay with me until she arrived, and I was glad I did not want to go back to my apartment alone.

Half an hour later, my pastor and his wife walked into the room, she held me and spoke soothing words to me, and then they prayed with me.

I felt better having them near; they were such dear people to me.

As soon as we got to my apartment, I went into the bathroom to get out of these clothes and shower, my skirt was tore, and my whole body hurt.

As I stood in my shower and let the hot water run over me, the tears at last escaped my body, how could this have happened, all of my life I have been careful in everything I did.

I didn't believe there was enough hot water in the world to wash away what my attacker did to me; I didn't think I would ever feel clean again?

The pastor's wife knocked on the bathroom door, "Dana, are you okay?"

Would I ever be okay again? I thought

"I will be out in a few minutes." I told her.

She had coffee made; I took a few sips it burned because I had a cut on my lip from his hand holding my mouth so tightly.

They both encouraged me to lie down and rest, reassuring me my mother would be here soon.

I felt so violated he had no right to do this to me.

My pastor's wife came over and sat with me.

"Dana in time this won't be as hard as it is right now, God is going to help you get through this, you will not always feel the pain and fear you are feeling right now, you can't let this maniac control your life, what he did to you was indeed horrible, but you are a

fighter, and you have God on your side. They will catch him and bring him to justice."

I knew she was right I couldn't let this man take away more then what he has already took from me by keeping me in fear.

I laid on the couch, while they sat at the kitchen table drinking coffee and talking very low.

I tried to sleep, but every time I closed my eyes I could see him on top of me and feel his breath on my face.

But I must have fallen asleep, because I woke to hear my mother's voice quietly talking to the pastor.

"Mom" I held out my hand to her "Oh honey I didn't mean to wake you"

She said as she came and took me into her arms.

I didn't cry I just rested my head on her shoulder; it gave me peace to have her so near.

We both thanked the pastor and his dear wife for staying with me.

"If you need us please don't hesitate to call us, we are here and want to help anyway we can, we will continue to pray for you Dana, we love you sis."

"Thank you both so very much."

After they left, Mom rocked me like she did when I was a little girl while I told her everything that had happened the tears consumed both of us.

"Dana please move back home, tomorrow you can give the school your two week notice, you can live with me until you get your own place and you can start all over and put all of this behind you, Oh honey please."

"Mom I can't leave in the middle of a school year, beside I can't let my kids down."

"Then I'm staying with you." She stated.

"Mom you can't do that what about Paul?

And besides, this is where I chose to live, when you tried to talk me out of it.

I will find a safer place to live, one without a package garage.”

And I promise as soon as the school year is over, I will move back home.

I want to move away from here, I will never go back into that parking garage, I have always felt very uncomfortable being in that garage even in the day time."

“That makes me so happy to know soon you will be back home, then maybe I can rest at night.”

We will find you a place with some security in it.

Okay let's get some rest, than we can talk to the school and let them know you will be off work for a while, than we are going to find you a safer place to live”

What time I am afraid I will trust in thee   Psalms 56:3

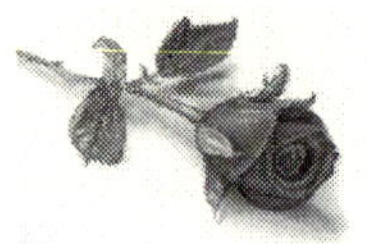

Chapter Three

I Talked to the principal of my school and told her what had happened, and I asked her to please keep it confidential, I didn't want my colleagues looking at me differently or with sympathy.

She was very sympathetic, I seen her wipe away her tears as I was telling her what had happen to me.

She was a very kind lady.

I also put my notice in I wouldn't be returning in the fall.

Sunday morning, mother and I went to church, I knew no one there would know the reasons Prayers were being asked for me, and I needed to be in church Where I could feel love from everyone there, just like I always have.

Church was my safe haven.

.After taking our seats someone tapped me on the shoulder.

"Hi, may I sit with you?"

It was Jeff, I had forgotten all about asking him here.

"Yes certainly,"

I moved down the pew closer to my mother to give him room to sit.

He seemed to really enjoy the church service and thanked me again for inviting him.

The pastor and everyone shook his hand and made him feel welcome, I heard him tell the pastor he would be back, and I was glad, Jeff was a sweet guy.

"So who is this Jeff?" my mom asked me on the way home.

"He is a teacher at my school, I had invited him to church, he is new in town, and he doesn't know anyone here yet."

" Well, he seemed very nice I like him."

The next day I filled out an application for an apartment is wasn't far from my school.

It was a lot more expensive then my old apartment, but it had a lot more security and no parking garage, it was also gated, and you had to know the password to enter the premises.

The lady called me the next day to say I could move in at the first of the week.

I could tell my mom had more peace of mind leaving me in this apartment.

The following Sunday, Jeff was at church again, he sat closer to the front, and as I watched him, he seemed to really enjoy the preaching, he held on to every word.

After the service, my mother invited him to have lunch with us, but all I wanted to do was to go home and finish packing, I wasn't ready to be out in public other than coming to church where I felt safe.

"Only, if I can treat." He said

Mom and Jeff did most of the talking at the restaurant which was fine with me.

I was busy checking everyone out that entered the restaurant, every guy I saw I wondered if it was him?

Jeff kept looking at me. "Dana are you feeling okay, you are quite today"

"Yes I'm fine just tired."

"Then I will not keep you ladies, thank you so much for inviting me to lunch this was nice."

"Jeff I couldn't help but notice you drive a truck, how much would you charge to move somethings for us?"

It was at that moment I wanted to crawl under the table and not come out.

"I would love to help you ladies at no charge"

Mom gave him my address and we left.

"Mom that was so embarrassing, how could you ask him that?"

"Why, what was the harm? Jeff is a really nice guy, and he didn't seem to mind helping us."

Mom, you put him on the spot, what was he support to say?"

"I'm sorry honey; I didn't mean to embarrass you."

"I know you didn't, I'm sorry I'm just on edge lately.

"Well you have every right to be, if you like I will call Jeff and cancel."

"No mom, it's Okay, he did act like he didn't mind helping us.

After School the next day, Jeff was there to move my things.

I still felt embarrassed I think because I liked Jeff and I didn't feel comfortable with him seeing or moving all of my things.

I stayed in the new apartment putting things in place while mother went with Jeff to get the last load.

Tomorrow mom and I would go back and clean the apartment and turn in my key and say goodbye to my nightmare.

After they returned and mom was out of the room Jeff asked me if he could talk to me.

"Dana, I was wondering if you were sick because I know you took some time off of work."

"No Jeff I'm not sick, I just needed some time off"

"Oh I'm happy to hear that, maybe while you are off, you would like to have dinner with me sometimes?"

"I'm sorry; I don't think so, but thanks for asking"

"No problem" I could tell I hurt his feelings, and I felt bad, so instead of me leaving him feeling like I didn't like him, I decided to tell Jeff what happened.

But When I told Jeff that I had been attacked in my parking garage the night I had met him at the restaurant.

He became very upset that he had not seen me home that evening he felt guilty.

"Jeff I didn't tell you to make you feel guilty, I told you so you would know the reason I couldn't go out with you as a matter of fact, right now I never want to leave my apartment again.'

"Dana, I hope you don't give into this fear, don't let this creep take away anymore from your life than he already has, by shutting yourself up in this apartment is punishing yourself and you don't deserve that."

"I know it's just so hard right now, I haven't told my mother, but I'm so scared of every little noise I hear.

I keep having nightmares of that night."

"I'm so very sorry this happened to you."

Mom came back into the room, so we stopped talking, I knew if I told her how I felt, she wouldn't leave me, and that wasn't fair to her.

After we got everything moved, I thanked Jeff for his help, as I turned to walk into my bedroom carrying a box I heard my mother say to him.

"Jeff I need to ask you a favor.'

"Of course" Jeff said. "I want you to keep an eye on my daughter for a while after I go back home."

"I was already going to do that." Jeff said. I walked in the living room.

"Hey you two I'm not a child."

"No you're not, but I'm doing your mother a favor, so don't argue with the adults." Jeff said with a laugh.

And he was as good as his word, after mother left.

When we were at school he would walk me to my car, tell me to keep the doors locked and every day I would have to call him to let him know I was home safe.

And I knew he was talking to my mom, keeping tabs on me, and it did make me feel better to know someone was watching out for me.

Every Sunday Jeff would take me to eat after church, usually with a couple from our church.

Some Saturdays we would get together with the other young couples and go out to eat and then bowling.

Jeff was always the life of the party he had made a good impression on the people at our church.

He was always doing something at the church from cleaning to building, they fell in love with Jeff, and I was scared I was doing the same.

It had been three months since my attack in the garage, try as I could everyday it came back to haunt me.

I knew I had to put faith over fear.

Mom called me every day; I knew she worried less knowing Jeff was taking good care of me.

Jeff did keep me busy. I knew it was to take my mind off of that night.

I stopped telling him when I would have a nightmare. I knew it made him feel bad for me.

There is no fear in love; but perfect love casteth out fear: because fear hath torment. He that feareth is not made perfect in love. 1 John 4:18

Chapter Four

But another nightmare was taking place in my life. I had missed three periods. First I was sure it was because of the drama that happened to me, but now I was getting worried.

The next day on my way home I stopped at the pharmacy and purchased two pregnancy tests.

I waited till the next morning to use it, and my fears were correct it showed positive.

I laid on my bed and cried, how could this be happening to me.

This meant that I was never going to be able to put this nightmare behind me, I could never move on with my life.

This would haunt me forever. I had to talk to my pastor.

I wasn't scared as I entered my car and drove to his house, I didn't call him first, I just went.

When he came to the door, the tears were already falling down my face.

"Dana, what is wrong?" he said with so much concern in his voice.

His wife came from the other room, she almost ran to me when she seen I was crying, she took me into her arms and lead me to the couch, "Sweetie what is wrong?"

"I'm pregnant" I cried.

"Oh no are you sure?" "Yes I'm sure." I could see them look at each other.

My cell phone had been bussing every few minutes I knew it was Jeff.

I knew I had to answer it or he would have a panic attack

"Hello" "Dana I have been calling you for a long time, are you okay?"

"Yes, I'm okay ""Oh thank god, you had me worried to death".

I came over to talk to the Pastor."

"Babe, why didn't you call me?"

"I just needed a woman to talk to, and I didn't want to worry my mom."

"So are you feeling better now?" I could hear the concern in his voice also.

"Yes I am thank you."

"May I speak to the pastor?"

"Okay, feeling a little confused I handed my phone to the pastor.

"Hi Jeff, yes she is a strong girl, she is going to be fine in time, Okay, see you soon Jeff."

When I took the phone back, Jeff informed me he was coming to escort me home.

"He loves you Dana very much Jeff is a good guy, and he is going to understand and support you though this ordeal…" pastor told me.

"I want to believe that, but why would he want to be with me now that I'm having another's man's baby?"

"Do you love him?" "Yes I think I do" I said

Then sweetie you are going to have to trust him"

"I know you are right but I also have another fear What If I can't love this baby, what if I resent it, what if every time I look at this child I'm reminded of that night?" I wept.

"You will love this baby, because you have Jesus in you, and we both know Jesus is love, This baby is part of you and you must remember that it is an innocent baby and had nothing to do with what

happened to you, this is your baby and he or she is going to have to have its mother to love and care for it, sweetie I promise as soon as you hold this little baby in your arms how it was conceived is not going to matter anymore."

"But the sooner you tell Jeff and your mother the better, you don't want you to do this all by yourself, you need your mother with you."

"I will but I want to wait and make very sure I'm pregnant."

His wife came and put her arm around me.

"Dana you are not alone in this, there are people who love you very much, and if you want, I will make you an appointment with my gynecologist."

"Thank you, I would like that then I will know for sure." I gave her a hug. "Thank you"

"I will call tomorrow and see if I can get an appointment for after school, one day this week.

Pastor opened the door for Jeff. "Hey how is my girl?"

"Better now that you are here." "That's what I like to hear." He smiled

After talking to the pastor and his wife for a few minutes, .Jeff followed me home then walked me to my door and gave me orders to lock my door.

That night I cried myself to sleep.

The next day at work one of my students came up and asked me if I was sick, she said I looked pale.

"Well I don't feel great but thank you for asking, but I will be fine.

I had a Doctor's appointment right after school; I was so hoping he was going to tell me I just had the stomach flu.

But instead he confirmed my fears I knew my plans never worked out but I never dreamed this is how my life would turn out.

I was done with crying I had to either make the decision that I was going to tell Jeff about the baby or I was going to stop seeing him and make myself get over him and I had to make that decision soon.

I'm just going to accept all of this and believe that god has a plan for me.

Come unto me, all ye that labour and are heavy laden, and I will give you rest. Matt 11-28

Chapter Five

I Spend the whole weekend at home when Jeff called, I told him I didn't feel good and I wasn't going to church the next day.

I spend the morning in the bathroom, throwing up.

I knew I had to tell Jeff I was pregnant and I knew when I did; I was taking a chance of losing his friendship.

When the school year was over I was moving back home, it would be before the baby was born. And there I would make the arrangements to put the baby up for adoption.

I have already put in for a transfer, even though there were no openings right now

That was okay because I wanted to stay low until after the baby was born, I asked Mom and Paul not to tell anyone I was pregnant.

After the baby was born I could substitute until an opening became available.

My pastor called me to see why I hadn't come to church and to make sure I was okay. He said he was worried about me, I told him I was having a hard time with all of this.

He told me he and his wife wanted to come over and talk with me.

I got dressed and dried my tears.

I was glad they were coming over I would tell them of my plans.

"Dana we know this is very hard, I wanted to tell you that Jeff came to speak to me yesterday, he is very worried about you, Dana he loves you very much, and I think you should talk to him soon.

Because the fact is, you are going to have this baby and God will make a way, you are not to blame for this, and neither is this child. But we also worry about you and I know if your mother and Jeff knew, you wouldn't have to carry this burden alone, so please think about telling them.

"I will talk to them very soon, but I have given this a lot of thought and I have decided

That at the end of the school year, I will be moving back home and when this child is born I will put it up for adoption"

"I think if that is what you wish to do, we will support you."

"Thank you, for being here for me and for caring about me."

After they left, I thought about what they said to me and I agreed.

I can't do this by myself I needed my mother.

I was very nervous when I dialed Jeff's number. "Hi Jeff" "Hi Dana, I was just about to call you" he sounded so chipper.

"Jeff could you come over I need to talk to you".

"Yes ma I will be right there."

I thought about how I would tell him, but when I opened the door and saw him standing there, all my rehearsed words were gone.

He took my hand and lead me the sofa "Dana I know there is something wrong, is it me? Do you want me to stop bugging you so much because believe me, It's only because I love you and I worry so much about you."

"No Jeff and you certainly don't bug me, Jeff I love you too.

I just realized this was the first time we had spoken of love.

"Jeff, there is something going on with me that I have to tell you.

Something that will most likely change our relationship and you might not want to see me anymore."

"Dana there is nothing you could say to me that would make me not want to see you."

"Jeff you know what happen to me almost four months ago"

"Yes I blame myself for that night every day."

"Jeff I know now no one is to blame, not me, and certainly not you, but the attacker himself.

Jeff that night caused more damage, then what he just did to me.

I'm pregnant."

At first he just stared at me, than he took me into his arms "Dana I'm so sorry you have to go through this, but you won't go through this alone I will be here every step of the way. I'm so sorry my darling" he held me and spoke soothing words to me like a child.

I knew I had made the right decision telling him.

The next day at work, I found a dozen red roses on my desk from Jeff, I was so lucky to be loved by such a sweet guy.

Right before school was out for the day, Jeff came to my room.

"Hey I'm picking you up at 6 o'clock for dinner" "Jeff I have so much homework to do tonight"

"See you at 6pm" and with that he walked away.

Okay was that an "I'm not taking no for an answer?"

After school I went home took a long relaxing bath and prayed I wouldn't throw up again to night while I was out to dinner with Jeff.

I was ready and waiting at 6:00 pm.

He took me to a nice restaurant and after wards we drove out to a lake and he held my hand as we walked along the water.

"Dana you know I love you?"

"I do know you love me, and I love you."

"Dana can I ask you a question?" "Sure"

"Will you please marry me?"

"Wow" I just stared at him, a million thoughts ran through my mind.

"Can I ask you a question?" "Anything" he said.

Are you very sure about this? I mean you know all the circumstances and you still want to marry me?"

"Dana, I don't care about the circumstances I care about you, and I want to marry you and help you raise this baby, because I love you."

"Jeff I'm not keeping the baby"

"That is your decision and I will support every decision you make.

"Oh Jeff I do love you and yes I will marry you."

"I promise you will not regret it, I promise I will make you happy, and I promise you will never have to fear again."

"That is a lot of promises." I said as I put my arms around his neck.

"Promises I intent to keep" he said as he carried me to the car.

"Let's go talk to our pastor" "tonight, isn't it kind of late? "No he is expecting us." "What? You already told him?"

"Well I had to talk to my pastor first."

We had a nice visit with the pastor and his lovely wife.

"If you two get married right away, no one would have to know the baby doesn't belong to Jeff." The pastor said.

"Even though Jeff and I will get married, I will still put the baby up for adoption, my decision on that hasn't changed."

"Oh I see, I guess I was thinking since you would be married, you would keep the baby,

But the decision is yours,"

"I do hope ,you two don't have bad feelings toward me for doing this, but I really feel like it's the right thing to do."

"No Dana, we do not, you are helping some loving couple out there that have longed for a child of their own to love. You are giving them a miracle.

So don't ever think we think bad of you, my wife, and I both think you are a very strong person."

"Thank you Pastor, that makes me feel better."

We thanked them for everything. Then Jeff took me home.

On the way back to my apartment Jeff and I made plans to go visit my mom and my step dad.

"We will leave Friday right after school, if that will work for you" Jeff said.

"I will be ready" after a kiss bye and instructions to lock my door he was gone.

The next day at school I called Mom to let her know we were coming for a visit.

She was either very happy I was coming home for the weekend or she was very happy Jeff was coming with me I couldn't tell which.

Lo, children are an heritage of the LORD: and the fruit of the womb is his reward Psalms 127:3-5

Chapter Six

Usually on my trips home it took forever it seemed, but not today.

Jeff turned a long boring car trip into fun and excitement we talked and made our wedding plans and for once I forgot about the last months of agony my life has been in, I was too happy to be sad.

When we arrived, mom and Paul were so happy to see me and they made Jeff real very welcome, I knew my mom really liked Jeff.

My mother and Paul had purchased a new Rv, their plans were to do some traveling, after Paul retired but so far it hadn't left the back yard.

Jeff would be staying there.

They took us out to Dinner then we went to visit Sara and Coy .and my niece and nephew.

Today I really missed my brother and Sandra, it has been four years since they passed and it seem like everyone's heart still grieved, their memories were everywhere.

It was so good to be home among my family it gave me a sense of safety.

After we got back to my mom and Paul's house I told mom we needed to talk to them

"Okay Dana let's go into the living room"

After everyone was seated I began.

"Mom, Paul I have two different kind of news so I will start with this one.

Jeff has asked me to marry him and I said yes."

"Oh my goodness this is awesome" I had never seen my mom get this excited before.

"Honey I'm so happy for you guys" after hugging me, she gave Jeff a hug.

"I must say if I could have picked your husband Dana it would definitely be Jeff"

Paul gave me a hug and shook Jeff's hand and told us congratulations.

After the excitement of that news was over I continued

"There is more"

"Oh I'm sorry Dana, I'm just so excited" Mom said

"Mom, I don't know how to tell you guys this so I'm just going to tell you.

When I was attacked and assaulted. The damage didn't stop there.

I'm four months pregnant by my attacker" and the tears were already falling down my face as I spoke.

Mom was on her feet before I could finish she took me in her arms "Oh baby I'm so very sorry, but you are going to get through this, you are strong and you have God and people who love you" she was crying as hard as I was.

Than Paul came and held me "I love you Dana and we are going to help you, don't ever feel like you are alone in this okay." "Thank you Paul, I know I will be fine because I do have God and my family and a wonderful man in my life."

"Oh honey yes you do" than she went and gave Jeff another hug "Jeff you are an extraordinary man to my daughter and God will bless you and Dana in your marriage."

Jeff had tears in his eyes.

"Can I call you Mom" "Certainly"

I could see the joy that he just gave her.

"Okay Mom I just want to say that god blesses me every day and he has blessed me when he gave me Dana and now this wonderful family that I can call mine, I don't feel extraordinary, I feel blessed."

"Thank you for taking care of our daughter, Mom said as more tears fell down her cheek.

"Okay this is a celebration. My daughter is getting married and I'm going to be a grandmother again.

I'm going to be happy about this innocent little baby that belongs to God."

"Mom, I'm not keeping the baby" I said and for the first time since learning I was pregnant, I felt sad about giving the baby up.

She looked at me for a few seconds before she said anything.

"Honey, you know we will support you in whatever you decide."

"Thank you Mom, now can we please talk about something else? I don't want the rest of our weekend to be spent in sadness."

After a few minutes of silence Paul jumped in with his news to save m and I was glad the focus would be off of me.

"Dana, you know I have a son?" "Yes I remember you telling me about him. Isn't his name Jayson?"

"Yes, he lives in Kentucky with his wife Anna and they have three daughters."

"Oh wow" I said.

"Next week, your mother and I are going there to meet them and to see my son, I haven't seen him since he was a baby.

"I'm happy for you Paul. I know you must be excited."

"Yes I am and a little nervous."

Mom came over and sat next to Paul.

"We have searched a while for Jayson, because his last name was not the same as Paul's last name that made it difficult to find him."

Mom sat there looking down at her hands that were folded in her lap, I knew she was in deep thought.

"Not meaning to bring up the subject again, but have you two set a wedding date?" she at last said.

This was the part I was trying to avoid telling my mother.

"Yes we have set a date April 12th it will be on a Saturday.

Oh that is not too far away, but we can do this,"

I could see the wheels turning in my mom's mind.

"Mom, we are only having a very small ceremony with just the pastor and his wife, you and Paul and hopefully Jeff's parents and sister"

"Oh I understand."

But I could see the disappointment in her eyes.

"Okay well what about the reception?"

"After the ceremony we will be going to a nice restaurant, Mom I know you had always planned on me having a big church wedding and so have I, but now that is not my priority anymore, I hope you can understand."

"Oh honey, of course I understand, you are marrying a great man, and that is all that matters."

"Thank you Mom" I went over and gave her a hug.

He that loveth not knoweth not God; for God is love 1 John 4:8

Chapter Seven

When it was time to leave for home it was hard for me to leave my mom.

I felt like my emotions were all over the place.

I was happy I was marring Jeff, but at the same time I was sad that my plans to move back home had changed.

Was I doing the right thing by marrying Jeff and was I doing the right thing giving this baby up?

I have always dreamed of my wedding day, my friends and I would talk for hours and look through hundreds of bridal catalogs,

My mother and I have talked about my wedding day so many times, and it was nothing like this.

I loved Jeff, but my life was not going as I have planned at all.

One of my plans was to move back home, I had never planned on staying in Chicago.

But of course my life hadn't gone by my plans.

In the bible, Paul said "He thought himself happy"

That is something I have been doing a lot of lately.

I knew I should be thankful, God has been good to me, and these things that I'm missing out on, are just material things and I should focus my life on spiritual things.

I can't forever dwell on my plans that didn't work out in my life.

But I have to make new plans, and my first plan was to get closer to God.

Maybe after the baby was born and in the arms of a loving mother, then could I get on with my life.

On the drive to his parents place, I started get a little nervous.

Jeff hadn't really talked much about his family, other than they lived, and worked on a farm, it was hard to picture Jeff growing up on a farm, but he said he used to milk the cows, feed the chickens and work in the fields.

He said his father was very upset when he left the farm and went to college.

He had one older sister, her husband had passed away a few years ago and she moved back home.

"What if they don't like me?" "Are you kidding, how could anyone not like you"

When we pulled up in the drive, a woman came out to meet us, she was short, and round and she wear an apron, with her graying hair up in a tight bun.

"There's my momma? He said as he got out of the car.

"Oh Jeffrey, I'm so happy you called to say you were coming for a visit, I have missed you" she said as she gave him a big hug.

"Hi Momma, I have missed you, I want you to meet someone, Momma, this is Dana."

"OH yes so very nice to meet you, my son has told me so much about you, the beautiful girl he is going to marry.

You are so pretty." She gave me a hug.

"Come in, you must be tired from that trip"

The house was an old farm house, but it was warm and cozy and smelled like fresh bread baking.

"Crystal, your brother is here, she yelled up the stairs.

A few minutes later, his sister came down"

"There's my brother that never comes to visit." She said with a laugh.

"Hi Sis, Crystal, this is Dana the love of my life."

My face turned red from his remark.

"Hi Dana, I was so shocked to find out someone hooked this brother of mine, you must be a very special lady."

"Hi Crystal"

His sister was beautiful she took after her brother she looked like she just stepped out of a vogue catalog.

Now I was curious about what their Father looked like.

"I hope you two are hungry, I fixed Lunch"

"You know I'm always hungry for your cooking, Dana, you are in for a surprise

My mom is the best cook in the world."

"Jeffrey you stop fibbing to that girl."

She laughed.

"Crystal, can you please go to the barn and tell your father, Jeffrey is here, and Lunch is ready please.

The four of us waited at the table for his dad for at least twenty minutes before we heard the back screen door slam.

Everyone seemed all tensed at his arrival.

He took his place at the head of the table without speaking, he started filling his plate with food, and I felt very uncomfortable.

He was tall and rugged looking with a very hard exterior like he was mad at the world, I could see why his family felt intimidated by him.

Maybe back when he was younger, he could have been a nice looking guy it was too hard to tell.

"The food is delicious Mrs. Smith"

"Thank you Dana, you are sweet."

"So Dad, how is everything going, how are the crops doing this year?"

"Don't act like you care about the crops or this farm, you don't have to make small talk with me, but since

you are, let me ask you a question, do you have a job yet?"

"Yes Dad I'm teaching school in Chicago,"

"So in other words No." he snapped.

Totally ignoring his statement Jeff said "Dad I would like for you to meet

Dana, we are getting married in April,

And we both would love it if you three

Could come to the wedding it is going to be just a small ceremony."

With his fork in mid-air he glanced up at me without saying a word.

He was the rudest man I have ever encountered.

"Jeffery, you know we would love to come, but there is always so much work to do here on the farm, we couldn't just up and leave son."

"I understand Mom; I know you guys have a lot work here running this farm." "But we do wish you two the very best," she sounded so sorry and a little sad.

Crystal never spoke it was almost like she was embarrassed for how her father acted.

Later after his dad went back to the barn, Crystal and Jeff went to walk around on the farm and I helped his mom clean up the dishes.

Afterwards I decided to go out and catch up with them as I got closer to the barn I could hear Jeff and his dad talking, or I should say Jeff was talking, his dad was yelling.

"Dad, you know I never wanted to stay here on the farm, this is your life, but it has never been mine..."

"Only because you may have to get your hands dirty and do a real man's job

You have always been lazy when it comes to work"

"Dad I'm not lazy, I just wanted to be a teacher, not a farmer"

"Teacher, that's a woman's job."

"I'm sorry dad, that I have always been a disappointment to you."

I could hear the emotion in Jeff's voice.

"You got that right." He showed his son no compassion and it made me sick.

I quickly turned and walked back into the house, I didn't want Jeff to know I had over - heard them talking.

On the way home Jeff was quite.

"Jeff, are you okay?" "Yes, why?"

"You just seemed quite, that's all, and can I ask you something?"

"Sure"

"Why is everyone scared of your father?" "They are not scared of him; they just want to keep peace with him."

"Has he always been the way he is?" "As long as I can remember."

"Why is he like that?" I hoped I wasn't asking too many questions"

"Dad thinks that whatever he says should go, he thinks he is right about everything, he is just very controlling.

And people should do as he says."

"Have you ever been close to your dad?"

Dana, no one has ever been close to my dad including my mother."

"I take it he wanted you to run the farm with him."

"Yeah, he already had my life planned out for me, and when he found out I had a mind of my own, he wouldn't accept the fact I had other plans for my life that didn't involve farming.

My whole life I wanted to be a teacher, so I studied hard to make it happen.

"Well I'm very proud of you." I told him, as I reached for his hand.

"Dana, you don't know how lucky you are to have a loving Christian family.

I know I have my mother and sister, but I have never had a father." He said.

I know how you must feel not having that relationship with your father.

My father passed away when I was only three and I don't really remember him, but what I heard from others, he was a great man, and I wished I had known him.

Beloved, let us love one another: for love is of God; and every one that loveth is born of God, and knoweth God1 John 4:7

Chapter Eight

Standing in front of our pastor with justhis wife and my mother and Paul there.

Jeff and I were married.

He insisted on writing our own wedding vows.

"Dana I promise to always love you and I promise to take care of you, and I promise to never break your heart but to protect it, I will always be here for you, you will never have to fear again, because I promise I will never let harm come your way again.

Jeff's words were sweet and I knew he meant well by saying them, but the reality was, he was making promises he could not keep.

I know it rains on the just and the unjust and I'm not exempt from this world's troubles.

But he still brought tears to my eyes.

At the restaurant Mom and Paul gave us an awesome wedding gift.

They had rented us a cabin in the smoky mountains for two fabulous weeks.

I was so excited I needed to get away for a while.

The next morning they drove us to the airport.

When we arrived at the airport, we once again thanked my parents for giving us this awesome gift and then we were on our way.

I rested my head on the seat and held my husband's hand.

How could life get better then this I thought.

Tennessee was gorgeous with the blue mist that hangs above the tall mountains

Our cabin was very rustic and I loved it. It was so peaceful here, we took long walks on the trails,

We sat on our little deck watching squirrels play sometimes we got to see deer come very close to the cabin.

We went into town and took historical walks and we heard the stories by our guide about the pioneers that had once lived here. I think the one that Jeff and I both loved was the little one room school house, the desk and little chalkboards that sit on the desk, which back then were called slates.

We went into a very old church that still had the original organ, we were told.

I stood in the doorway and I tried to picture the many services that were held here.

My heart felt at ease that whole day, I didn't think about my problems.

After our tour was over, we were free to roam around all the little buildings.

But our favorite one was the little schoolhouse, we went back into it and Jeff would pretend he was a school teacher from way back then, with his not so good southern accent, he was so funny, he would have me laughing all day. Then afterwards we would go back to the cabin and Jeff would start a fire in the fire pit, we would roast hot dogs and marshmallows and then later we would sit on the porch and look at the stars, I was very contend just staying like this forever.

But all good things must come to an end, before we knew it; it was time to go back home to life and the real world.

Beloved, let us love one another: for love is of God; and every one that loveth is born of God, and knoweth Go He that loveth not knoweth not God; for God is love. 1 John 4:8

Chapter Nine

SItting in that room waiting for my appointment, I knew I had to talk to my Doctor today about the adoption details, I wondered what she would think of me giving the baby up.

She knew everything that had happened to me.

I had told her at my first visit.

"Dana" the nurse called my name. I walked into the examining room, and took a seat. Only a few minutes had passed before Dr. Jenkins came into the room.

When I walked out of her office that day, I felt better and I knew I was doing the right thing, Dr. Jenkins told me there were a lot of couples out there that couldn't have children, and I would be giving them a miracle.

I wanted my baby to have a loving couple, someone to love and care and protect this child and would love it unconditionally.

Six more weeks this would all be over, and I could go back to my church and School would be starting soon, no one there knew that I was pregnant except the principal; I just have to stay inside my home from now on until after I gave birth.

When I got home Jeff had cleaned the entire house and fixed dinner, he was so good to me. We never talked about the baby, but I think Jeff was glad I had decided to give the baby up for adoption, and I didn't judge him for that, just like he didn't judge me.

My pastor and his wife came over once a week to give us a bible study, I really enjoyed them.

When I got close to my due date, my mom came to stay with us, and I was so happy she did.

Because the closer to the due date, the more scared I became.

I had told my mother and Jeff my wishes and they said they understood.

I wanted them to stay with me right up until it was time to give birth, then I wanted them to go downstairs to the cafeteria, I also wanted time to myself after the baby was born.

I didn't want them to see the baby and have that picture etched in their minds forever.

I really enjoyed having my mom here, we talked and played games and a few times we drove out of town for lunch and shopping, I was going to miss her after the baby was born and she went back home.

Late one night I awoke with back pains, but after Jeff gave me a back massage it eased up and I went back to sleep.

But before morning the pains were worst, Jeff woke mom up and we went to the hospital.

Thy sat with me and Jeff rubbed my back and fed me ice chips until it was time they gave me the epidural.

Then they left the room as I had requested.

I heard her cry, but I didn't see her. They took her away very quickly

I couldn't stop crying, I cried for myself for the baby for my mother I hoped one day I would get over this ordeal, I felt like I was doing the right thing not just for me but for this little baby also, she deserved more then what I could give her.

The doctor told me she was healthy and that is all I needed or wanted to know.

After a few hours had passed,

Jeff and my mom came in and we all three held each other and cried.

I needed them I found out very quickly I didn't want to be alone.

I got to go home the next day to start my life over.

A week later I went to church everyone seemed happy to see both of us.

By the time School started back I was ready for it, I had missed the children.

I tried to pretend like everything was okay, but it wasn't the smile I wore now was fake.

They were all shocked that Jeff and I were married and I think the other teachers were a little jealous.

Jeff didn't joke around with them as before.

Life was good but the only thing missing was that little baby girl.

I thought about her every day, was she being took care of? Was she okay?'

I needed a change in atmosphere

I needed to move back home to be around my family.

But I couldn't ask Jeff to move it wouldn't be fair to him.

I tried to make the best of everything and just take one day at a time but I had notice Jeff didn't attend church like before, He didn't stop going, he just didn't go as much, he seemed so restless.

I told myself I was worrying over nothing.

One evening, he was sitting at the table grading papers and I was ironing, he just threw all the papers on the floor and stood up.

"Do you feel better?" I asked.

"Dana, Are you happy?"

"What do you mean?" "I mean are you happy with our lives, because I'm not!"

I'm sick of this god forsaking city.

Sick of this tiny apartment I need a change, we need a change, before we both go crazy here,

Do you ever wonder why we don't make plans for our future we have never even talked about buying a house.

We have been married for almost three years, and it's like our life is on hold. But on hold for what? So we can just give up and die in this rut?"

"What do you want to do?" I was almost to scare to ask.

"I don't know, a move, a different job something"

"A different job?

Maybe a move, but I love teaching."

I said shocked he would even suggest changing jobs.

"No I don't mean that I love teaching also, I mean what about if we both try to get transferred somewhere else" "Are you saying maybe another school, or another state?" I was already getting excited.

"Another state, we could go to your home where your family is"

"Oh my goodness Jeff ,are you serious? I would love that." I almost started jumping up and down like a kid.

"Then let's finish out the year, but in the mean time we put in for the transfer and have your mom start looking for us a house."

"Oh Jeff, You have just made me so happy" I said as I gave him a big hug.

"Hey didn't I promise I would make you happy," "Yes, you did, and you have"

We didn't waste any time, we put in for our transfer the very next day, and gave our notice we wouldn't be back the following school year.

We both knew the chances were very slim we would get a teaching job right away, but Jeff would get a job somewhere until then.

All week at School my whole outlook on life changed, I felt joy and I felt hope.

I no longer wear a fake smile but my smile was very much real now.

After the kids had gotten finished decorating their class for the Christmas party I let them open their gift from me.

The school Christmas programs were awesome, I knew I was going to miss my students.

On Christmas break, before Jeff and I left to go to mom's I called Jeff into the bedroom.

"Hey I have something for you." I handed him a small package.

"What is this, I thought we were not opening out gifts until Christmas morning."

I know but I wanted you to open this one while we were alone.

I could see the confused look on his face when he pulled a baby's toy out of the little box.

"Are you having a baby?"

"No, we are having a baby" I laughed.

"Are you happy?" "Dana, you could not have given me a better Christmas gift." He gave me a long hug.

"We better get on the road before it gets dark"

Once we were on the road Jeff could not stop talking about the baby, he was so happy.

"What about names?" "Jeff don't you think it's a little soon to be picking out names?"

"No, my son is going to have to have a name"

"What about your daughter?" "My daughter also."

Mom was so happy we were moving back home, she said the same thing Jeff said.

We couldn't have given her a better Christmas gift.

We had a wonderful time on Christmas day, with Mom, Paul. Sara, and her family. And I finally got to meet Jayson and his family.

"Hi Jayson, I had heard so much about you, and I'm so happy to meet you."

"All good things I hope." "Well of course" I laughed.

"Dana, this is my wife Anna." "Hi Anna, I'm glad you guys came to spend Christmas with us."

"Oh we are so happy to be here," Anna was very

outgoing and nice I liked her right away.

"This is our oldest Courtney" "Hi Courtney,"

Courtney was tall and very pretty.

Then he continued to introduce his other two daughters, Becky and Ariel.

Ariel had long red hair like her mother, while the other two girls had dark hair like their dad.

"You have beautiful hair Ariel." I told her.

"Thank you." She shyly said.

"That is how she got her name, because of her red hair." Anna said.

Once we were all seated for our beautiful Christmas dinner,

Jeff stood up to make an announcement,

Dana and I would like to tell everyone how thankful we are to have a family that has prayed for us and that has cared for us, and we are both looking forward to moving here and going to church with everyone, we want to give God the glory and the thanks for bringing us here.

And we also would like to say that in the summer" Jeff reached down and took my hand before he continued.

"There will be another little person in this family."

"Oh my goodness, this is the best Christmas, Congratulations you two.

And thank you for making me a grandmother again."

After hugs and congratulations, we started on this delicious meal.

It was the best Christmas I had since I was a little girl.

And I hated to see it end, but Christmas break was over, and so was our little vacation.

All during my pregnancy, I thought of my daughter, I wondered about so many things.

Jeff was so happy that he was going to be a daddy.

I knew he was going to be a good one.

He was always bringing me little things, he was a great husband.

We had decided we didn't want to know the sex of our baby until it was born.

But I hoped it was a boy for Jeff.

Just before the end of the school year Jeff got a fifth grade teaching position in my home town, we were both so excited.

"Great is our Lord, and of great power: his understanding is infinite." Psalms 147:5

Chapter Ten

I Was so glad our baby would be born in my home town where I was born, but most of all being with my family.

As I was packing our things for our move I felt like I was leaving my first baby here and that made me sad.

If I just knew she was okay maybe I could rest better.

I prayed god would somehow let me know my baby was being took care of and that she was loved.

Our Pastor was very supportive of our decision, he had been praying about this with us, and felt like being around my family and going to church with them was good, he knew how much I missed my mother.

Six months later after a tearful goodbye to my students and with a small u haul we were on our way home, with so many hopes for our future.

I felt like my plans were at last coming together.

We would live in mom's camper until we found a house.

I loved being close to my mother again, going to church with her.

On our first Sunday there, everyone was so happy to see us, and everyone made us feel so welcome.

Jeff took a job as a night watchman, so we could save more money toward our house.

I didn't like Jeff working over nights, but I knew right now we didn't a choice if we wanted out of this RV and it was just until school started back in the fall.

More frequently I was having dreams about a baby; they were all almost the same.

I was running down a street and it was raining and I could hear a baby crying but I couldn't find it.

And it was during one of those dreams when something woke me , looking at the clock I saw it 4:16am, I knew my water had just broke, I got up and went into the bathroom, the baby wasn't due for two more weeks.

I called my mother.

"Mom, sorry to wake you, but Jeff isn't home yet, and I think my water just broke"

"Okay I will be right there" I was glad I was right in her backyard.

On the way to the hospital, I called Jeff.

"Hello" "Hey are you ready to be a daddy today?" "Wow are you sure?" he sounded worried.

"Yes my water broke" "Okay I'm on my way home" "Jeff we are on our way to the hospital so come there, and don't worry I'm fine."

Five hours later I gave birth to beautiful baby girl.

As I held her, I couldn't help but cry thinking about my now three year old daughter.

Did she looked like her, I never held her, I never seen her and now I regret that, I regret giving her up and I have for a long time.

Mom came over and put her arms around me, "You are thinking about her, aren't you?"

"Yes mom I always think about her, Mom I have made a horrible mistake, and I can't fix it, I should have never given her up."

"I pray for her every day, and I'm trusting god that she is well and happy" My mom said.

"Mom, do you think badly of me for giving up your granddaughter?"

"No I don't, you felt like you were doing the right thing, and I stood behind you."

They had taken the baby down to be weighted and Jeff went with them.

"So have you and Jeff decided on a name yet?"

"Yes as of a matter –of- fact, we would like to give her your middle name Lynn"

"Oh thank you" "and I have always liked the name Katie."

"Katie Lynn" I already loved the sound of that name. Mom said.

"So Do I"

"You know you were named after your grandmother"
"Yes I know"

"We are back" Jeff said as he pushed the little bed into the room with the nurse walking in behind him.

"Isn't she the most beautiful baby in the world?" Jeff said "I think so" Mom agreed.

"Oh no this little girl is going to be spoiled rotten" I said as I rolled my eyes at both of them. But I had to agree she was beautiful.

Katie was a good baby, and a joy to have, I loved her so much I couldn't imagine my life without her and Jeff I'm sure felt the same way.

One night I woke to find Jeff out of bed, I went in the other little room where we ad Katie's bed and found Jeff standing over her bed crying.

"Jeff what is wrong?" "Nothing is wrong, she is just so beautiful, and I can't believe this little human is my daughter."

I put my arms around him." Well I'm glad it's you that has the postpartum depression and not me"

I joked. "Let's go back to bed; she will be up soon enough.

Blessed is the man that trusteth in the LORD, and whose hope the LORD is. Jeremiah 17:7

Chapter Eleven

When Katie was eight months old, I received a second grade teaching position at the elementary School I had attended when I was a child. It was going to be strange teaching there, I didn't like the idea that I would be starting at the end of the year. But the other teacher had a sickness and just couldn't stay until the end of school.

But at least I had a job and now Jeff could quit his night job and just teach, and we could start looking for our house.

Mom was more than happy to care for Katie.

"Hey Mom, here she is all fed and changed, she should fall back to sleep in a little while".

Mom laid Katie in her little bed, she had got for her. "You have time for a cup of coffee?" "Oh no sorry, Teacher can't be late on her first day"

"I read in the paper that a young woman was attacked somewhere around the collage last night." Mom said. "Oh no did they catch the guy?" "I don't think so. It didn't say.

Just keep your doors locked"

"I will mom, okay got to go, I will call you later"

Memories tried to enter my mind, but I stopped them, I had a new job today and I couldn't let what happened to me almost four years ago take over my thinking today.

But again I thought of that precious baby that I gave up, she was my daughter, and I didn't even know her name.

I prayed every day that God would let me know that she is well and with a loving family and that she is happy.

I was so happy I now had a job.

I hadn't realized how much I had missed teaching.

These little second graders were darlings they had so many questions for me.

Today was just a getting acquainted day, I allowed them to share stories with the class, and I shared stories with them. I let them rearrange the class room so everyone got to be seated somewhere new, it was a fun day.

But tomorrow would be our first real school day with their new teacher.

I missed Katie and couldn't wait to see her. This was my first time being away from her.

There is no fear in love; but perfect love casteth out fear: because fear hath torment. He that feareth is not made perfect in love. 1 John 4:18

Chapter Twelve

The week went very good, the children were all surprised to know this very room we were in. I also attended second grade here.

They thought that was hilarious, and they couldn't picture me being a little girl and in this room.

Even though the desks had since been replaced. I showed tem where my desk used to sit.

That gave them more questions for me.

Jeff was teaching across town at the middle School.

I didn't see a lot of him during the week.

I was happy when Jeff put in his two week notice at the night watchman job, he never had time to sleep and he was tired all the time and moody, all he wanted to do on the weekends when he was off of work was sleep, I felt like he was growing distant from me, and I didn't like it.

So now he could spend more time with me and Katie.

And I hoped now he would have more time for church.

"Jeff, they are having a married couple night at our church Friday night.

Mom said she would watch Katie, I would really like to go."

"I would really like to take you" he said as he took me in his arms.

It felt good to have my husband back at home at night with me and Katie.

After school on Friday I stopped by my mother's house to give Katie a kiss good night.

"Dana, if you want Katie can just spent the night here, that way you guys don't have to be in a hurry to get home afterwards."

"Thank you mom, but we don't plan on being out that late, and I feel bad because you have had her all day.

"I love having my granddaughter here." "Well if we are late coming home, I will call you."

"Okay have a good time"

Jeff hadn't got home yet, so I took a bath and got dressed, I wanted to look nice, and so I wear a new outfit and curled my long hair.

Jeff and I never do anything together, so I was excited to be hanging out with the other couples at our church.

I had been ready and waiting for Jeff for almost an hour before I called his cell phone.

"Jeff where are you? The party starts in an hour."

"I know I'm sorry, I had a flat tire and I'm changing it now, I will be there as soon as I can"

"Okay, honey, I'm sorry.

Another hour passed, so I called his cell again, I was getting worried.

"I'm on my way" he sounded out of breath so I knew he was trying to hurry.

By the time he got home and showered and dressed, we were going to be late, but I didn't care I still wanted to go.

But not after another hour had passed and Jeff was still not home.

I called mom to let her know, I was coming to pick up Katie.

"Why aren't you two going? I don't understand"

"Jeff still isn't home, first he said he had a flat, but that was three hours ago an hour and haft ago he said he was on his way home.

I'm sure this is his way of getting out of going to the church."

"Dana, I'm sorry"

"It's Okay I will get over it, thanks for watching Katie."

When I got back home, Jeff's car was in the drive, and he was in the shower.

I changed Katie into her Pajamas and then I changed into my night clothes.

I was sitting on the couch feeding Katie, when Jeff came into the room.

"Why aren't you dressed?" He sounded so shocked.

"Jeff I'm sure the party at the church is over by now."

"I'm sorry Dana; some things just can't be helped."

I didn't want to be mad at Jeff but I just couldn't help it.

The next morning, before he was out of bed, I went outside to look at his car and just like I thought, the spare tire was still in the trunk of his car, not on the car.

Why had he lied to me? And where had he really been?

I went into the bedroom and yelled at him.

"Jeff when someone has a flat, don't they usually put the spare tire on the car?"

He sat up and looked at me,

"You playing Nancy Drew?"

"Jeff where were you?"

He got up and started getting dressed.

"I didn't want to go to that couples thing, so I just drove around for a while."

"Are you serious?, you couldn't have just said you didn't want to go?"

"No because I didn't want to disappoint you."

"So instead you lied to me?"

"Dana I know I was wrong and I'm so sorry."

I just walked out of the room before I said something I would to repent over.

I didn't speak to Jeff all day, he tried to do little things for me to make up for what he did, but it didn't work with me.

Sunday Morning he was up and dressed for church before I was out of bed.

And then after the service, he asked Paul and mother if they would out to eat with us.

Mom could tell I was still upset with Jeff.

All week I made him think about what he did, I wanted him to feel bad.

I can do all things through Christ which strengtheneth me. Philippians 4:13

Chapter Thirteen

The following Friday I went to Mom's to pick up Katie.

"Dana, did Marty get in touch with you?"

"No why?" "He said there is a house right down the road, you know the one

The Harding's used to live there, it's been vacant for a while now, but Marty said they just listed it at a very low price"

"Oh wow, that would be perfect, I will tell Jeff"

After telling Jeff, I tried to call Marty but found out he was away for the weekend

"We can just talk to him at church Sunday" I told Jeff.

Marty was a good friend and a good realtor.

Sunday morning after I got Katie and me ready for church, Jeff was still sitting at the table.

"Jeff we are going to be late." "I'm not going today, I will go tonight."

"But we were going to talk to Marty'

"Just talk to him and get all the details.

I turned my face before he could see my tears and walked out the door with Katie.

When I took my seat beside mom, she asked where Jeff was at. "At home"

She didn't say anything more.

After the service was over I found Marty.

"Hi Dana, so did your mom tell you about the house right down from her?"

"Yes she did.

I know which house you are talking about, and I like the neighborhood and I love the big yard.

"Well I know they are eager to sell because they are moving out of state, the house does need lots of work, but it has a lot of potential if someone knows anything about remodeling. And you won't beat the price."

"When would be a good time to look at it?"

"How about tomorrow afternoon?

I could meet you guys there around four."

"That will be fine, Thanks Marty we will see you tomorrow."

The next day mom watched Katie while we looked at the house.

Marty was right It needed a lot of work and I could see Jeff turning up his nose on a lot of thing, I could tell he wasn't liking what he saw.

But I could also see a lot of good potential and the price was a lot lower than what we were willing to put on a house.

After telling Marty we would get back with him, we went to Mom's to pick up Katie.

"Dana that house needs way to much work and I'm not a carpenter."

"But the price is so low" "I know but by the time we pay someone to fix it up it will be way over what we can afford."

"So what did you think of the house?" Mom asked.

"After Jeff filled her in on all the things wrong with the house, Paul started asking him questions about things.

I had forgotten that Paul was a contractor.

After they talked more about the house Paul asked if he could take a look at it.

So I called Marty right away and set up an appointment for the next day.

Paul went through the house with his chipboard writing things down he even climbed up on the roof and crawled under the house. It took him a while.

Back at the house he had some good news for us.

He told us the foundation was very good, the roof and plumbing and electric was fine, the only thing we was looking at was the exterior of the house and these things were very easy to replace all the walls just needed painted. He said we could put down laminate floor though out the house and he could get us all the kitchen and bathroom cabinets at his price.

But best of all he said he would help us do the work.

Jeff called Marty and put down a lower price than what they were asking.

And they accepted.

We were now home owners.

So every day Mom took care of Katie and we worked on the house.

By the time School was out for the summer. We were moved in and our house was beautiful. Thanks to Paul...

I was so happy to be in our house and it wasn't a moment too soon, I just found out I was having our second child.

Jeff was thrilled.

We decided to wait before telling anyone about our new addition until after the holidays.

I loved decorating our new house for Christmas, my life was perfect now.

I had a home walking distant from my mothers, I had an awesome church, a husband, our jobs, our beautiful daughter, and now God has blessed us with another child.

We had a Christmas get together at our house.

Jaden was seven months pregnant with their second child but she was still so stylish and beautiful.

"How is everything Dana?" she said as she sit down beside me.

"Everything is good" "Jaden, you did an awesome job with the children's Christmas play this year."

"Oh thank you, it did turn out great."

"So have you found if you will be having a boy or girl yet?"

"A girl, I'm so happy because this will be our last one, so now we will have both. And she will have Momma's name

Sandra Marie" "Awe that is so sweet"

I know you miss your mother."

"Yes I do, very much."

After everyone had left Jeff was helping me clean up.

"Jeff I want to tell mom about the baby"

"I thought we were waiting a while"

"I know but, I can't wait anymore."

"Okay, then tell her" he laughed.

A few days later I invited them for supper.

After we had eaten, we went into the living room and I took Katie into the bathroom to clean her up and I put a tee shirt on her that read I'm going to be a big sister.

"Katie remember, just play with your toys and don't tell Okay?' Okay, mommy I won't"

I had to laugh because twenty minutes had passed and neither one of them even noticed Katie's shirt, so I thought I would see just how long this would go before one of them noticed.

I saw mom looking at Katie as she played with her toys on the floor.

"Katie, sweetheart, come here please, as Katie was walking toward her grandma, Mom's eyes got so big. And she looked over at me.

"Are you having a baby?"

"Yes" "Oh Dana, I'm so happy, congratulations you two, or I should say you three. " Katie did you know, you were getting a baby brother or sister, and you didn't tell grandma?"

"Yes" she laughed.

"Three years ago on Christmas you told us about Katie, you sure know how to give good Christmas gift.

"For God hath not given us the spirit of fear; but of power, and of love, and of a sound mind." 2 Timothy 1:7

Chapter Fourteen

Katie was learning so much about Jesus in her Sunday school class.

When she would talk about it to me, I would wonder about my first daughter, was she learning about Jesus also,

I prayed she was.

The night mares about that night in the parking garage has stopped but the dreams about hearing the baby cry still haunts me.

One night we were getting ready for bed when Jeff told me he was going back to night watchman.

"But Jeff, why would you? we are doing fine."

"Dana, I don't want to be just fine, I want to be above fine."

"Jeff I need you her with Katie and I and now the baby."

"I will just work for a little while there and I will be home every night by ten pm. It won't be so bad, and I will put the money I make toward a new truck, you know we need a different vehicle."

I knew he was right, I drove a new car, but his was on its last leg, so will you quit once you can buy a truck?"

"Yes I will, promise."

During the evenings Katie and I spend a lot of time with mom, after I would get home from School we would shop for the baby's new room, time went by very quickly.

I was hoping the baby would wait until the school year was out, but he had different plans.

I called my mom one evening, because

I was having pains, and she came over.

I called Jeff around eight thirty to let him know we were going to the hospital.

But I got no answer we took Katie to Paul to take care of her, I kept trying Jeff's cell on the way to the hospital but still no answer.

After the nurse connected the monitor they were monitoring the baby's heart beat and I could tell something wasn't right, because she went out of the room and came back with another nurse.

After a while, my Doctor came in and checked.

A little while, the Doctor checked me again he looked at the monitor for a long time studying the long white papers.

"Dana "Your baby is showing signs of distress, which means he is not receiving enough oxygen.

I want to do a C-section right away because you are even close to delivery.

Mom kept trying to get Jeff but with no luck.

When I awoke from the surgery,

Jeff was there.

"Good morning Beautiful"

"Have you seen the baby?" I sleepily asked.

"Yea he is beautiful "

Jeff said with a big smile.

"Jeff where were you?"

"Dana, I'm so sorry I wasn't here for my son's birth, but I took off early from work because a guy that works there told me about a truck so we went to look at it, I didn't know it was almost two hundred miles from here or I wouldn't have went with him, I'm so sorry"

"So did you buy it?" "No I didn't, it was not what I was looking for."

At that time a nurse came in with the baby.

He was so tiny, he looked like Jeff.

I was so proud of him.

"Now we have a daughter and a son, we are so lucky." Jeff said.

"Jeff where is mom?"

"She said she wanted to give us time alone, but she will be back a little later."

Jeff held the baby, he had such love in his eyes for his son, and it melted my heart.

"Andrew fits him perfect, doesn't it?

" I said.

"Yes it does Andrew Adam Smith"

"I know it made mom happy when I told her I was given him Dad's middle name."

Two days later I went home from the hospital, mom helped me out a lot with the baby until I got back on my feet.

Katie loved her new baby brother and wanted to do everything for him.

I was waiting until Andrew was six months old before I went back to teaching, I didn't want to go back in the middle of the year.

When Katie was four, we put her in preschool. She loved it she was a very smart little girl.

Andrew followed her around everywhere and wanted to do everything his big sister did.

My children were my joy.

Philippians 4:6 - Be careful for nothing; but in every thing by prayer and supplication with thanksgiving let your requests be made known unto God.

Chapter Fifteen

I Love the new School year everything was so fresh and new, the kids were excited, coming in wearing their new outfits with their new book bags.

This year I was getting two new students, it is always exciting for me to see new faces in my class room.

This was my fifth year teaching at this school, so I have grown very close to everyone at the school, my kids that went to the next grades I still got to see them occasionally.

I let the kids talk and get acquainted with each other before calling the class to order most of them already knew each other because they were in first grade together.

"Mrs. Smith, guess what?" Ashley said to me. "I have no idea what?'

"We are getting a new a girl and she smells bad, and her shoes are torn"

"Well thank you Ashley, you can be seated now please."

"After getting the class seated and I had their attention, I did the name call to make sure everyone was present, than I allowed each child to tell the class

Something they did during their summer break, as we were doing so, the principal tapped on my door, I opened the door to see she had two small children with her, a boy, and a girl. "Well hello, we have been expecting you, please come in."

"Good morning Mrs. Smith, I would like for you meet Taylor he will be in your class this year,

Taylor, this is your teacher Mrs. Smith. "Hi" he slyly said.

I just stood there I couldn't believe my eyes I was looking at an older version of Katie.

"Mrs. Smith, are you okay?" She was asking me. But I couldn't take my eyes off of the little girl that was half hidden behind the principal.

"I'm sorry, Hi Taylor welcome to second grade.

I knew the children were not related. Taylor was dressed in the finest, when the little girl was dressed in rags.

"Taylor, this will be your desk, after he took his seat, I turned my attention back to the girl. "Mrs. Smith this is Bethany, and she is a little shy"

"Hi Bethany, that is a beautiful name, would you like to come in and meet everyone, I reached for hand.

"Mrs. Smith, we will talk in a little while." "Okay" I said, I already knew it would be about this child.

I knew I had to do my job today and push my feelings aside, but she looked just like Katie, they could be twins, and every feature was the same. My Katie had long beautiful blond hair, while Bethany had the same blond hair, it was just matted, my heart was crying.

But I managed to pull myself together. I kept telling myself this was impossible, she can't be the baby I gave up seven years ago, but despite my logic thinking, somewhere deep down, I knew I had just met my daughter for the very first time.

After taking Taylor and Bethany to the cafeteria and getting them settled with their lunch, I went into the principal's office to find out all the information she knew about her.

"Hi Mrs. Thomson, can you tell me about the new student Bethany Jameson"

"Oh yes I wanted to talk to you about her, I know the way she is dressed is not good and I have spoken to her father, he said when he gets paid he would buy her some shoes.

I also told him her hair had to be brushed and she had to come to school clean from now on" "Where is her mother?" I asked. "He said her mother passed away three years ago, and that he has been raising her alone, plus I think he may have a drinking problem, because I could smell alcohol on him, I have a feeling things are not going to work out very well with Bethany and her father, because something is just not right, and I will be keeping my eyes on her and him I want to make sure this little girl is not being mistreated in any way." Because I can already see she is lacking the proper care, she is much neglected and I don't like what I see."

"May I ask, what is her birthday?"

She looked at kind of strange before she looked into the file that was still on her desk.

"December 19 2000"

"Thank you Mrs. Thomson" I walked back to the cafeteria.

Even though the birthday was not the same the year was.

I just knew she was mine, I felt it and I wanted to take her home with me and take care of her, I had to find out.

The other kids kept their distant from her, she did indeed smell, but it wasn't her fault.

I was waiting for Mr. Jameson, when he came to pick up Bethany from school that day.

When he pulled up he didn't bother to get out of the car, so I walked up

The car window, holding Bethany's hand

"Hi Mr. Jameson, I'm Mrs. Smith, Bethany's teacher this year, how are you?"

He looked at me with glassy eyes; I could tell he had been drinking.

"I'm fine, get the car girl, he said to Bethany. " Mr. Jameson, May I ask you a few questions?" " If it's about how she is dressed I have already told the principal

I would get her some shoes when I can"

"No I was wondering if it is okay with you, if I could give Bethany some clothes and shoes."

He just looked at me for a few seconds, then threw his hand up in air and said "Suit you." Then he drove away.

I hated to see him drive away with her, somehow I was going to prove she was the one I gave birth to seven years ago, and I was getting her back.

After work I called Jeff to tell him to pick the kids up from mom's I had an errand to run, glad he didn't ask questions.

I went shopping I got her five outfits, shoes and a book bag and under garments.

That night after the kids was in bed. I told Jeff I needed to tell him something.

He came into the living where I was seated going over everything in my mind what I would say and not sound foolish.

"Okay just hear me out before you say anything."

"Okay" he said.

Jeff today I got a new student in my classroom, and I think she is my daughter, she looks just like Katie, I mean just like her."

"Okay wait a minute that is crazy, just because a kid looks like Katie doesn't mean she is your daughter, everyone has a look alike"

"Jeff I know she is, I feel it, the mother passed away three years ago, I have to find out for sure, Jeff this little girl is much neglected.

I went after school and got her clothes, she was dressed in rags, and she needs me."

"Stop it Dana! Listen to yourself.

If you want to buy her clothes that is fine. But you have got to get

This out of your head, she is just your student, and nothing more."

Jeff has never raised his voice at me, I knew he was upset.

But I didn't care, I had to find out if she was my daughter, I couldn't live with myself knowing now what I know now.

I can do all things through Christ which strengtheneth me. Philippians 4:13

Chapter Sixteen

The next morning when Bethany came in, she was dressed in exactly as she was dressed yesterday, I'm sure she slept in her clothes.

I had already had permission with Mrs. Thomson to get Bethany cleaned up today, she send down an aid to take over my class for a few minutes.

I took Bethany into the girl's locker rooms and gave her a shower and washed her hair, after her hair was dried and tangled free it was beautiful just like

Katie's, she looked like a new kid in her new clothes and I could tell it made her happy.

I knew I had to make friends with Mr. Jameson, if I was to ever find out anything about them.

I waited outside with Bethany, for him to pick her up. He was almost an hour late.

"Hey sorry I'm late, get in the car," He told Bethany.

I knew I had to talk fast.

"Mr. Jameson, are you from here, or have you just moved here to our little town?"

"We just moved here" "So how do you like it so far?

"It's like every other state."

"Oh where are from originally?"

I got to go, get in the car girl" he acted like I was annoying him.

It bothered me that he didn't even call her by her name.

When I went to moms to get Katie,

I told her everything; she was a lot more supportive than Jeff was. "Honey, we got to find out and I will help you anyway I can,

first thing we need to do is talk to Pastor Hays, because we need the church to be praying about this, because believe me prayer can open doors."

"But what about Jeff, he wants me to drop it' "Are you going to drop it?"

"No, I can't, he just don't understand she could be my child."

"I know and she could be my granddaughter"

Every day when Mr. Jameson picked Bethany up from school I would try to befriend him but he was a hard man, and I did not like him.

Every time I would try to talk Jeff into helping me find out if she could be the baby I gave away, he would get upset with me.

At church I would request an unspoken prayer, the pastor told me he would try to help me find some things out, and he also told me he was worried about Jeff, even though he didn't work nights anymore, He still missed a lot of church he came up with a lot of excuses why he couldn't come to church.

So when I got home, I came right out and asked him

"Jeff, can we talk?' " Okay, Dana let's talk" he sarcastically said.

"Why are you missing so much church, is there something wrong?'

"Okay can I ask you a question, Dana?" "Yes, you can ask me anything,"

"Are you still pursuing your student," "What do you mean?"

"You know exactly what I'm talking about, you have it in your head she is your long lost daughter, and I want you to stop, and then maybe I will start going back to church"

"Okay wait a minutes it has been virtually one week since I met this little girl so Jeff I know that is not the

reason you have started to miss church, this has been going on for a while."

"Jeff, why is this bothering you so much?'"

"Why? Are you kidding, we have a family and I thought you were happy,

but you are asking me to help you get someone else's kid and raise them, we have kids we don't need another one."

"But Jeff, she is not just a kid I truly believe she is my daughter, why can't you understand that"

"Dana seven years ago, I was glad you gave the baby up, I didn't want to raise a baby that belonged to you and another man, why can't you understand that?"

He walked away.

I was glad he walked away so he wouldn't see me cry.

I decided tomorrow I was just going to ask Mr. Jameson if Bethany was adopted, I had to know.

But I didn't get that chance, Bethany didn't come to school, when I asked Mrs. Thomson If her dad called, saying she was sick or something, she said no, she hadn't heard anything.

When she didn't come the next day, Mrs. Thomson called him to check on her.

Around ten o'clock, Mrs. Thomson came to my room.

"Dana, can I talk to you in the hall please" "Yes, okay class, continue on your paper."

I walked out in the hall.

"Before I had a change to call Mr. Jameson, I received a phone call that

Mr. Jameson was involved in an accident, he was drunk and Bethany was in the car" "Oh no" I cried. "She is okay she has spent the night in the hospital and she will be placed in a foster care for now, they said she would be going to another school.

What hospital?" I asked "they didn't say" "Do you know what foster care?

"I don't know that, they were just letting us know she wouldn't be returning to school." "Thank you Mrs. Thomas" She had no idea my suspicions.

It was so hard to concentrate on my class. I was so worried about Bethany.

Somehow I had to find a way to prove she was my daughter.

And get her away from that man.

"Casting all your care upon him; for he careth for you." 1 Peter 5:7

Chapter Seventeen

I knew I couldn't talk to Jeff about this, so I talked to mom, I hated going behind Jeff's back but I couldn't just drop this like he wanted me to.

Katie was now in kindergarten and her class was down the hall from my class room,

When I was walking down the hall to collect Katie, I thought about my family and how blessed I was, and Bethany deserved to be a part of my family not living in foster care or with a man that didn't even act like he loved her.

When I gave her for adoption, I thought she would be with a loving family.

I felt like God was giving me another chance and I was going to take it.

When I got to Mom's I told her the whole story, she said she would call around and see what she could find out, I was so grateful I had my mom on my side, I needed someone to talk to about this and I needed help.

"Hey, I was beginning to worry about you guys," Jeff said as we walked in the door.

"We went to grandmas to get my brother," Katie informed her dad. "Oh you did? Well where are my hugs?" Jeff opened both arms and they ran to him, they loved their father.

And again it made me think of Bethany, she deserved so much better than what she had, she deserved a family, and I knew her adopted father didn't care for her.

I cried and pray every night for God to please make a way for me to get my daughter back, and to please protect her.

"Hey Babe, I'm going with Paul tomorrow to help him fix a roof, he said it should take a few hours, you didn't have plans did you?"

"No, that's fine, me the kids will hang out with mom tomorrow"

In my mind I thought, this is prefect, hopefully mom has found out what hospital Bethany is in and I can go see her.

The next morning after feeding the kids, we drove to grandma's house.

"Hi Dana, I wanted to call you last night to tell you what I found out but I didn't want to talk to you about it with Jeff, being home, so I asked Paul, to ask for his help today."

"Oh mom, you are a genius,I gave her a hug.

"Here is where she is, but you better go now." "Okay: I will hurry."

The hospital wasn't that far, but when I got there I was told I couldn't see her.

Unless I was a family member, I explained to her that I was her teacher.

But I still couldn't see her.

As I turned to leave, the nurse said to me "she wasn't hurt just scared and she is getting released today.

"May I ask you if a family member will be coming for her?"

"I'm sorry Ma'am, I can't tell you that."

"Ma'am, you said you were her teacher?" "Yes I am."

"I know that her social worker will be here soon if you would like to wait and speak with her."

"Thank you so much." I took a seat in the waiting room; I hoped she wouldn't be long, because I didn't want Jeff to make it home before I did.

I knew he would be very upset with me for doing this.

I could understand he didn't want to raise another man's child, but why couldn't he understand she was also my child and she didn't ask to be born.

I felt like she was all alone in this world, a world I brought her into.

A few minutes later a woman walked in carrying a briefcase and I was sure that must be her, she walked up to the front desk and the nurse was telling her something, than she walked over to me.

"Hello, I was told you are Bethany's teacher." "Yes I am. My name is Dana Smith." " Hi Dana, I'm Miss Daniels, and I'm happy to meet you, can we talk?"

"Yes" I followed her to a room with a long table and chairs.

"Please have a seat."

"Can you tell me if Bethany has any family members? Her dad will be away for a while, this is his second DWI, but this time he was also charged with child endangerment. He has told me Bethany's mother had passed away three years ago.

and there were no family members, but I just wanted to make sure he was telling the truth, because sometimes if there' a family dispute, the parent may not want to mention that family member."

"I wish I knew, but I don't, but I need to tell you something, and I hope you understand and can help me, but almost eight years ago I was attacked in my parking garage one night, and a pregnancy came out of it, I gave birth to a daughter, and I gave her up for adoption, when Bethany walked into my classroom, I knew she was the baby I gave up, I have a five year old daughter and Bethany could be her twin."

"Mrs. Smith, it has never came up that Bethany was adopted."

"But Mrs., Daniels, what if she was, and I'm her mother?"

I wish I could help you but because you gave that right up.

Mr. Jameson is her legal parent, even if he is not a good one, you should get an attorney because unless we can contact another family member, Bethany will become a ward of the state and placed in foster care."

'Okay, that is what I will do, thank you Mrs. Daniels."

As she walked out the door she turned and looked at me.

"Dana, can I ask you a question?" "Yes" I said. "Have you always regretted giving your baby up?"

"Everyday" The tears fell down my face. She smiled and walked out the door.

And it shall come to pass, that before they call, I will answer; and while they are yet speaking, I will hear. Isaiah 65:24

Chapter Eighteen

I Knew I had to talk to Jeff now, because I had to get an attorney, and I needed his help.

"After he got home and we had finished supper, I let the kids go outside to play, while I talked to Jeff.

"We have to talk." I don't know why I was so nervous to talk to my own husband.

"Okay, about what? Jeff I know you are going to be upset with me, but please try to understand, yesterday Mr. Jameson, Bethany's father was in an

accident and Bethany was in the car he was drunk."

" Oh my goodness, is she alright?"

He looked concerned. "Yes, she is fine. She was released from the hospital today, and she will be going into foster care, and Jeff, I can't let that happened."

"Dana, you do not know that this kid is yours, you can't go by just your feelings."

I could tell he was getting angry, But I wasn't backing down, Bethany needed me to fight for her now, and that is what I intent to do.

"How do you know all of this anyway?" He asked.

I went to visit her in the hospital today. I couldn't see her, but I did get to talk

To the social worker."

"Dana you need to start paying more of your attention to your own kids"

"Jeff if you could just see her, she looks just like Katie, but she has sadness in her eyes, she lost her mother *when she was only four years old, she has an alcoholic for a father, and she lives in poverty, and you asking me just to forget it?*

Jeff I need your help in this, I need you to support me and to help me pray about this little girl." I started crying. "Dana, I will help you pray for your student, because I can tell she definitely needs prayer, but I will not pray that she comes into our home, but that the lord will provide her with a loving family."

He put his arms around me and held me as he talked.

"Jeff, are you going to give me a hard time if I get a lawyer?

"Dana, I'm begging you, don't do this." "I'm sorry Jeff I can't live with myself

If she is my daughter and I didn't do anything to help her, she needs me."

"No Dana, Your family needs you."

Jeff went to church with me the next morning, we had an awesome service, and God gave me strength.

I told my pastor what I had found out and about Jeff; he said he would talk to Jeff.

"Dana I have been praying about this situation, and I just want to say, if it were my little girl that was being mistreated

There is not a rock I would not over turn to get her home. And I'm praying Jeff will come around because you guys need to be together on this."

"I agree and that is what I want, I need Jeff." "Yes you do" He said.

Walking into Mrs. Thomas's office the next day, I prayed she would understand and not judge me, for giving my child up, but now I had no other choice but to tell her the truth, because I needed her help.

"Hi Dana, how is your day going?' " Mrs. Thomas, I need to tell you something"

"Okay, it sounds serious, Take a seat" She motioned toward a seat across from her desk. After I told her everything, she was very sympathetic with me and

told me she understood now about Bethany and how worried she was also about her. She told me she would help me anyway she could.

"What I really need is a few days off."

Take as much time as you need I have two substitutes that want the hours, I will take care of it."

Blessed is the man that trusteth in the LORD, and whose hope the LORD is. Jeremiah 17

Chapter Nineteen

Sitting in the Lawyer's office, I had wished so very much that Jeff would have changed his mind and came with me, I didn't want to go against him on this and I hated it when he was mad at me, but I just couldn't give up and I believe that God was opening doors for me.

"Mrs. Smith, you can go in now" the receptionist said to me.

"Hi, Mrs. Smith, have a seat. Well, I know a little about why you are here,

But why don't fill me in on everything."

"Mr. Wilson eight years ago I was raped, and the guy was never brought to justice

And I became pregnant, I gave my baby up for adoption, I had a girl, and I have regretted it ever since. I'm married now and I have two children.

I'm a second grade school teacher, and at the beginning of the school year a new student was put into my class room, and I knew the first time I saw her, she was my daughter, she looks identical to her sister, and she was born the same year as the baby I gave up, her adopted mother passed away three years ago and she lives with her adopted alcoholic father, which was in an auto accident four days ago and the child was in the car, she wasn't injured I was told by the social worker.

He is now in jail for two DWI's and child endangerment.

She was put in foster care, and I'm here today to see if you can help me get my daughter back."

"Well first of all Mrs. Smith even though I do believe in Mother's intuition,

Unfortunately the court does not.

I can sympathize with your feelings of maybe thinking this could be your daughter, and if indeed it was to turn out she was your daughter, you gave up your parental rights eight years ago, and the courts will look at that."

He stopped to look at his papers on his desk. "Mr. Jameson is her legal father now."

"So can I have a DNA test done to prove that she is my daughter?"

"Well as I said, even if she is your daughter, you gave up parental rights.

And you would have to have the father's permission to have that test done."

"So are you saying there is nothing I can do?"

"I'm saying in most cases the rights of the adopted parents must first be legally terminated, before you could even consider getting your daughter back."

I thanked him for his time, but I didn't walk away feeling defeated, because I knew god was in this.

I called my pastor to see if I could talk to him.

I told him what the lawyer said.

"Sister Dana, what if we went and talked to the father and told him your suspicions, because you know maybe with him knowing that he will be servicing time, He might consider giving her back to you if the test proves she is your daughter.

"How would I do that, don't you have to be on some list to go and talk to someone in jail?" "Sister, I'm on that list, I go once a week to talk to the inmate, how about tomorrow at four pm? It's worth a chance, we will trust the lord to deal with Mr. Jameson's heart before we arrive."

"Thank you so much, that sounds like an awesome idea, because he has to know she will stay in foster care and surely he doesn't want that."

Later at home. I told Jeff where the pastor and I were going tomorrow, and what the plan was. He didn't seem too happy with the idea, but he didn't say anything.

"I was reading Katie and Andrew

A bedtime story that night when Jeff came into the room to kiss the kids goodnight, He looked at me and said. "When you are done, here, we need to talk"
"Okay" I said.

I had a feeling he was going to try and talk me out of going to the jail tomorrow to talk to Mr. Jameson, but my mind was made up. I wasn't going to desert my daughter again. I wouldn't stop until she was home with her family.

"You want a cup of coffee?" I asked Jeff before we started talking.

"No thank you, I'm fine" After pouring me a cup I sat down on the couch facing my husband.

"Dana, please hear me out, I have been thinking about this and I feel like I have come up with a solution that will work for our family." "I'm listening," I said.

"I will help you every step of the way to get your student out of foster care, if you give up this foolish notion that she is your kid, and we will try to find her a good loving home."

"Jeff, she is not a puppy in a pound, she is my daughter and why do you keep referring to her as my student?"

"Because Dana, that is what she is. As much as you want to believe she is the baby that you gave up eight years ago, that is just crazy thinking and I believe you have never forgiving yourself for giving your baby away and you are trying to ease that quilt by pretending you can fix the past if you could fix this little girl, but even if you end up raising this kid. Your

daughter will still be out there somewhere and by doing this you will have done none of your children any good.

"I will be doing Bethany Jameson good."

Dana, you are doing this for selfless reasons and you are not considering anyone in this family, you are not giving us a choice, or asking us how we feel about it, Are we even a family anymore Dana?'

"Jeff that is not fair, you know I can't discuss this with a five year old and a two year old.

I don't expect you to understand, you didn't carrying the baby or give birth to her, but every day since I signed those papers I have been sorry, and just what if Bethany is really mine, should I just give her away again?"

"Dana, I told you I would help place her into a good home."

"Jeff as far as I'm concerned this is her home."

I went to bed and cried myself to sleep, when I awoke the next morning,

Jeff was sleeping on the couch.

I went into the kitchen to put coffee on, before waking the kids.

"Will you forgive me" he said as came up behind me and put his arms around my waist.

"I'm sorry too, I hate it when we fight, Jeff are you going to be okay when I pursue this" "Dana, I guess it doesn't matter what I say."

"For God hath not given us the spirit of fear; but of power, and of love, and of a sound mind." 2 Timothy 1:7

Chapter Twenty

I Was so nervous walking into the jail, I just wanted to turn and run.

After going though security, we were lead down a hall and into a room.

Mr. Jameson was seated at a table there was an office there also.

We sat across from him. "Hey I know you, your Beth's teacher, what are you doing here? Is this your husband? "No this is my Pastor"

“Oh I see you came to redeem me” he said with a laugh.

‘Mr. Jameson, I’m here to talk to you about Bethany.’

“What about her?” “You are aware she is in foster care?”

“Yea, So?” “Do you want her in foster care, Mr. Jameson?” “Look Ma’am Does it really look like I can do anything about it, at least she has somewhere to stay until I get out of here.” “How will you provide for her when you get out?” “The way I have always have, do you go to this trouble for all of your students?”□

“Mr. Jameson, can I ask you a question?” “What would you like to know?”

“Is Bethany adopted?’ “ What, where did you get that idea? Did she tell you that?”

“No she didn’t” “Than why would come here to ask me that?”

"Mr. Jameson, seven years ago in Chicago I had a baby girl and I gave her up for adoption, and I have been sorry ever since, and now I had another daughter and Bethany looks just like her, and I was wondering if maybe Bethany was my daughter also she was born the same year as the baby I gave birth to" I was crying when I didn't mean to.

He just looked at me, at first with compassion on his face, than he laughed.

"Lady you sure do have a wild imagination, but he didn't take his eyes off me, like he was searching my face for a resemblance of Bethany.

"Excuse me sir," my pastor spoke up.

"I would like to give you this, he handed him a bible and this is my church card.

If you ever want to talk, please don't hesitate to call, we will be praying for you."

He got up and walked back into another room with the officer, without a word.

As we walked out, my pastor assured me not to give up.

"I believe that his daughter was indeed adopted by the way he acted."

The pastor told me.

"I don't know what to do now."

"We pray and believe that god will open the door for you to walk right in."

Later at home Jeff didn't ask how it went today, I knew he didn't want to talk about it, so I didn't bring it up.

"So Dana went do you go back to work" "next Monday why?"

"I was thinking we could get away this weekend, take the kids somewhere"

"Okay if you want." I haft heartily said.

After I dropped Katie off at school, Andrew and I went to moms, I needed to talk to her.

"So tell me what happened yesterday?"

"Mom I don't know what else to do, he said Bethany was not adopted, Mom what if I have made a mistake?"

"Do you feel like you have?

"I can't explain this but Mom, I know she is my daughter, I just know it, and it bothers me so much that Jeff won't stand with me on this, I need to find out, and I can't rest until I know."

And now he wants to go away for the weekend, I know it's just to distract me, and he can't understand that I'm not just going to forget her."

"Honey, this is hard for Jeff this little girl might belong to you but she doesn't belong to him. And he doesn't want things to change."

"I know your right mom. I guess I need to give him a break, maybe a weekend away will do good, , but I won't stop trying to find out if Bethany is the same little girl I gave birth to seven years ago."

"I know you won't and I don't want you too, if she is your daughter, she needs to be with you, and I'm praying for this little girl, no matter what the outcome is."

"Thanks mom."

"Call unto me, and I will answer thee, and shew thee great and mighty things, which thou knowest not." Jeremiah 33:3

Chapter Twenty One

The drive was nice just the four of us getting away for the weekend, I was really trying to put all of my thoughts into my husband and kids and making sure we all had a good time, it was hard for me to put Bethany on the back burner for a few days, but for Jeff's sake I knew I had to.

Katie was so excited to be going to the children's arts and museums. I'm pretty sure Andrew was excited because his sister was excited.

He was a joy to watch as he imitated his big Sister, Katie was a good sister to him, but sometimes little brother got on her nerves because he wanted to do everything she did.

At two years old, he did have a little of his own personality.

At first he didn't adjust very well when Katie went to school full time, he didn't understand why he and grandma didn't pick her up at lunch time anymore.

Jeff took my hand as we followed close behind the kids and smiled at each other as Katie would explain to her brother all about the historian exhibits of fossils she would try to quote from memory from what she was told just a few weeks ago when she was here with her class on a field trip, Andrew listened intently.

After a day at the museums, we were all getting tired, after eating supper the kids were more than ready for bath time and then bedtime.

Jeff and I sat out on the terrace with our coffee enjoying the beautiful scenery of the night lights.

Jeff soon broke the magic with just a few words.

"Dana what do you think our future holds?" "What do you mean?" I had no clue where this conversation was headed.

"I mean where do you think our lives are going to be in a few years?"

"Jeff, are you trying to tell me something, because quite frankly I have no idea what you are asking me"

"Dana do you plan on continuing your search to find out if your student is your kid or not?" His words were very harsh.

"Jeff, I love you very much and I'm not trying to go against you in this, but please try to put yourself in my place. Yes, I gave my baby up and I have regretted that decision,

Jeff you don't know the many nights I have cried for my child and have prayed for god's forgiveness and if Bethany is my daughter, she is not with a loving family that I thought she would be with when I signed those papers.

She lost her mother and was with an alcoholic father for the last three years, and now she is in foster care, she has no one and you are asking me to once again turn my back on my baby and walk away. Jeff she is only seven years old.

And I'm sorry I can't do what you are asking, I have to know if she is my daughter or not."

The tears were now falling down my face.

"Okay so what if she is your daughter, than what? Do you just put your family in jeopardy to get her back?"

"Aren't you being a little dramatic, why would that put my family in jeopardy?

She doesn't belong to a mob?"

Jeff stood to his feet "Dana if you decided to pursue this, than our marriage is in jeopardy." Than he waked back into the room, I just sat there I couldn't *believe he said that to me, so If I didn't walk away from Bethany, my husband was walking away from me.*

Rejoicing in hope; patient in tribulation; continuing instant in prayer; Romans 12:12

Chapter Twenty Two

On the ride home Jeff and I didn't speak, and the kids napped for the most part and I was glad, I was so hurt that I didn't want to talk to anyone, I just wanted to go home and avoid Jeff as much as possible until he apologized to me.

I was not only hurt I was mad and being a little stubborn, I knew god wasn't pleased with me for that and I had to change my attitude.

I just couldn't believe he put me in this situation, I prayed he would change his opinion

About this and come to realize how much this means to me.

I loved Jeff and I couldn't imagine him leaving me, but On the other hand I couldn't live with myself if I didn't pursue my serve to find out if Bethany was my daughter.

I have prayed over and over about this, and I trust god to lead me.

When I got home I called my mother to ask her if she would like to go to the park with me and the kids, I had to talk to someone.

"I'm taking the kids to the park, be back in a little while, I didn't wait for his reply.

Sitting on the park bench with mom, I told her what Jeff said to me.

"Oh honey, I'm so sorry I know this has been tough on both of you, but I don't agree with Jeff and it upsets me that he told you that.

I know your marriage is stronger than that, he just spoke out of haste.”

“But Mom what if he meant what he said.” Am I doing all of this for nothing? I don’t even know how to find out if she is mine, every road is a dead end,.

every time I call the social worker, she tells me the same thing, she can’t tell me how Bethany is doing because I’m not family, I even asked her what if I became a foster parent? She said that was a good idea, but she couldn’t recommend Bethany being placed with me because of the emotional connection I have with her.

“Dana, we just have to let God work this out, I know he will make a way, he is the only one that can open a closed door for you, just try to be patient with Jeff, he loves you.”

“Thanks Mom”

“Dana Can you guys come for supper tomorrow night?”

Oh I'm sorry, but Jeff works two nights of the week at the college, Monday and Tuesday

"That is fine how about Saturday evening?"

"I will ask Jeff but I don't know if we will be good company or not."

"That's okay, maybe Jeff needs to be around family right now I invited Sara & Coy also.

And it shall come to pass, that before they call, I will answer; and while they are yet speaking, I will hear. Isaiah 65:24

Chapter Twenty Three

Jeff was at work, and I had just got the kids settled at the table for supper when I heard the doorbell.

"Pastor Hays, come in, what a surprise" "Dana can we talk in private please?"

"Certainly, Katie I will be right outside talking to the pastor, please help your brother."

"Okay Mom, I will help him."

"Is this about Jeff, missing so much church?" I asked

"No Dana, Tim Jameson called me this morning"

"What did he want?"

"It seems as if he has been charged with yet another crime, he got into a fight with an inmate and stab him in the neck with an object, not sure with what, but they will be moving Mr. Jameson to another facility very soon, and the reason he called me, he has asked to speak to you right away.

"Oh my goodness do you think he knows I'm Bethany's mother? I mean why else would he want to speak to me?" I couldn't stop the tears.

"Dana, we don't know the reason yet"

Ignoring his reply, when can I see him?'

"Tomorrow at five pm" he said.

"Okay, will you be going with me?" I just couldn't hide my enthusiasm.

"If you like, I will go with you, I really wish you could talk Jeff into coming also."

"I will talk to him and ask him, but there is something you need to know.

Jeff has told me if I pursue this, he said he would leave me."

Pastor Hays looked stocked "what?' I can't believe he would leave his family over this, Dana are you sure that is what he meant?"

"He didn't come out and say the words but I knew what he meant."

"I will talk to Jeff, this can't be right."

"Thank you Pastor"

"I will stop by Thursday if that is Okay?" to talk to him."

"Thursday is fine, Thank you"

Okay I will be back Thursday around five o'clock but don't let him know I will be dropping by, because I'm getting the feeling Jeff doesn't want to speak to me right now, because he hasn't been coming to church."

"I won't say anything to him "I will take the kids to my mother's.

That will give you a chance to talk to him privately and thank you again Pastor,

I do appreciate everything you have done for me."

"You are welcome."

I walked back into the kitchen to catch Andrew throwing his food to the floor

"Mom, Andrew threw his peas all over the floor" "it is okay honey, I will clean them up, let's finish our supper so you two, can get your baths."

My thoughts where everywhere, I didn't know how I was going to make it until Friday wondering what Mr. Jameson was going to tell me or ask me.

And how was I going to tell Jeff, should I wait until Pastor talks to him or should I tell him now, either way he was going to be so upset.

I felt I had to tell him now or he was going to think I was holding this news back from him, and that would just upset him more.

After the kids were in bed, I called mom, I told her what Pastor Hays told me, and she agreed that I should tell Jeff right away.

So I walked the floor waiting for Jeff to come home, going over and over in my head what I was going to tell Jeff, I prayed he would be reasonable and not give me a hard time about going and talking to Mr. Jameson.

I was so worried that he was going to get mad, but what other choice did I have, I had to find out what Mr. Jameson wanted to speak to me about.

Jeff was late getting home.

I laid down on the couch and fell asleep; I didn't even hear him come in until he said my name.

"Dana what are you doing up? Go get into bed it's late."

"Jeff why are you so late?' " The guy that works the grave yard shift was late, and I couldn't leave until he got there."

Jeff already sounded irritated.

I waited up for you, because I have something to tell you."

"What?"

"Mr. Jameson called Pastor Hays today and asked for me to come and see him; he said he wanted to speak to me."

"Who is Mr. Jameson?"

"It is Bethany's dad, you know that"

"Hey I don't remember the guy's name, what does he want to talk to you about?"

"I don't know" Pastor and I are going Friday to find out."

"No Dana, I do not want you going back to that jailhouse, talking to him."

"Jeff the pastor will be going with me, I have to know what he wants."

"I said NO!" Then he walked into the bedroom.

I followed him into the room.

"Jeff I'm sorry you feel this way, and I don't understand your reason, but I will be going Friday, because I need to know."

He walked passed with me with his pillow in his hand and closed the bedroom door behind him.

I was so torn, I felt like he was being very unreasonable and I prayed Pastor Hays would be able to get through to him.

I knew my marriage was in trouble, but if Bethany was my daughter, I was not leaving her in foster care, I knew it was my fault she was there.

She deserved so much more. She deserved to be with her family.

I didn't mention to Jeff that Pastor Hays was stopping by Thursday.

It didn't matter he wasn't speaking to me anyway.

Thursday he got up at noon, and I tried to be as nice as I could to him.

"Good morning, would you like some lunch?" "Nope" was his only reply.

I walked back into the kitchen to finish preparing the kid's lunch.

I didn't want to get into another argument with him so I decided to just stay out of his way.

"Mom, when will I go back to School?"

"When the summer is over sweetie."

"But I want to go back now to see my friends"

"How about we go to grandma's today and to the park?"

"Yay, Can we go now?" "Soon, Okay."

At four O'clock I told him I was going to visit mom, he didn't reply so I took the kids and left.

When we arrived, Mom had already arranged for Paul to take the kids to the park, so we could talk.

"Mom what do I do if Mr. Jameson tells me Bethany was adopted?"

"Then you will get as much details from him as you can, and go from there."

The attorney and the social worker both told me because I gave up my paternity rights, I am not her mother anymore, and I have no right to her what so ever"

"But what if Mr. Jameson gives her back to you?"

"I don't know?" but I pray to God he does."

"Dana hasn't God always come through for you?"

"Yes mom he has."

"Well let's just leave it in God's hands"

We held hands and we prayed. I felt so much better.

"It's after five; do you think the pastor is there yet?"

"I'm sure he is.

He has always been right on time,"

My mother said.

I had butterflies in my stomach just thinking about what I would face when I got home, hopefully Jeff wouldn't know that I knew Pastor Hays was coming over to talk to him.

At six thirty I went home when we walked in Jeff was lying on the couch reading a book, the kids ran to him, and he started playing with them.

He seemed to be in a good mood which I was so thankful.

"I will have supper done soon" he didn't answer but continued wrestling with the kids.

A few minutes later Katie came into the kitchen and said Daddy had to go somewhere.

"Did Daddy say where he was going?" "No he just said he had to go."

When supper was done and Jeff hadn't returned I called his cell phone, but no answer.

After supper I sent the kids to their rooms to play and I called pastor Hays.

"Hi Pastor, sorry to bother you, but I wanted to know how it turned out with your talk with Jeff today"

"Hi Dana, well it seemed that Jeff is very much against you trying to get your daughter back."

"But why? I don't understand" I said.

"He just told me he wouldn't raise another man's child that you had with him.

In fact he is very strongly opposed to it, I did ask him why he told you if you proceeded with this that he would end the marriage.

He just said Dana knows how I feel and if she chooses this child over our marriage, than it is her decision, and yes the conclusion will be the end of our marriage.

Dana, I don't agree with Jeff, but you need to know that he may leave in the end so this is something you need to take into consideration."

"Pastor Hays, I have taken it into consideration, but I also have to take this little girl into the same consideration."

"If Jeff loves me he is not going to leave me."

"I understand completely, and I feel strongly God is working this situation out and that he is opening up doors."

"Thank you Pastor for trying, I will meet you at the jail Friday at five O'clock.'

"Okay Dana, we will be in much prayer for you and your family."

As I waited for my pastor to arrive, I prayed and ask God to open up a door for us today,, and to give courage no matter what the outcome was.

As we were seated across from Mr. Jameson, I noticed how bad he looked and I felt sorry for him.

"Thank you for coming Mrs. Smith.

"You wanted to speak to me Mr. Jameson?"

Without answering me, he began to talk.

Remember ye not the former things, neither consider the things of old. Isaiah 43:18-19

Chapter Twenty Four

I *had it all at one time in my life, I owed my own business, a beautiful wife that I adored and a daughter, but life is funny, one day you find yourself complaining about the smallest thing like the weather, and then one day, your whole life can change.*

We were high school sweetheart, Jennie, and I; she was my life, three years after being married and trying over and over to have a child. Jennie was told she had cervical cancer and she had a complete hysterectomy.

It broke her heart to know she would never bore a baby, even though my Jennie was enough for me.

It broke my heart to see her hurt, so we decided to adopt.

I knew Jennie would be a great mother, and she deserved a baby to love.

We lived in Chicago and believe it or not we were told there are many girls in Chicago that have babies and give them up, we never knew her real birthday but she was born in 2000.

But I know it is you, because when we asked about the father, we were told he was unknown and the mother was the victim of a rape, Jennie didn't care where the baby came from.

She fell in love with Bethany, the minute she laid eyes on her.

For the moment he had started telling us his story his eyed were downcast, but now he looked up at me.

"And I know she would not want Bethany in a foster home just like I know how disappointed she would be in me, and I can't fail her again.

With tears falling down my face because I knew for sure she was my daughter I asked him about his wife.

"When Bethany was just three years old, Jennie's cancer came back.

I lost my beautiful wife and with her I lost all hope of living, I started to drink , I lost my business, I lost our home, I didn't care about anything or anybody anymore and that is why I'm where I am today.

"Mr. Jameson you still have God and he can help you." My pastor said.

"I didn't ask you here to speak of myself or God.

I asked you here today to find out if you still want the test and the girl?"

"Mr. Jameson I don't need a test, I know in my heart Bethany is my daughter."

I took Katie's picture out of my wallet and showed him.

"This is my daughter..."

"Wow, they looked like twins,

I remember when My Jennie would dress Bethany in those ruffle dresses and bows in her hair."

"Mrs. Smith I have talked to a lawyer about Bethany, and I have told him I wanted to sign my parental rights over to you.

He is looking into it."

"Mr. Jameson, I thank you so very much."

"I'm doing this for my Jennie."

"Bethany will be loved and cared for I promise you."

When we got outside I let my tears flow freely while the pastor patted my back.

"Now what?" he asked. "Now I talk again to my attorney and I beg Jeff to help me, because if I'm going to adopt her I need Jeff on my side."

"Okay, if you need me, I'm here to help you and like I told you before, we are in much prayer for you and your family."

"Thank you Pastor, I do appreciate all of your help."

I thanked God all the way home, for bringing Bethany into my life, for making a way, even when I couldn't see one.

I knew I had a giant to face when I told Jeff, but I also knew God didn't open this door to close it, God was on my side, and that's all that mattered.

I waited until the next day to tell Jeff, once he was out of bed, I fixed his breakfast while he showered and dressed.

I was sitting at the table when he came into the kitchen.

"Where are the kids?" "They are with Mom, Jeff we need to talk."

"Dana, every time you say we need to talk, it's the same old subject, and you know I have already told you how I feel and by talking about it repeatedly is not going to make me change my mind.

"Jeff, you have stated your feelings to me and yes I got it, now hear my feelings.

I love you very much, and it would kill me if you left me, I have tried to keep peace with you, but you see I have a little girl in foster care, and how can you think for one moment that if I was just to walk away from her as you have repeatedly suggested I do.

How do you think our lives would be any easier? Jeff I could never be happy again, I would worry constantly about her, and I would hate myself for abandoning her again."

"Then why did you give up almost eight years ago?" He snapped at me.

"Jeff I made a mistake, but I never dreamed my baby would be in foster care.

I thought she would be with a loving family."

Jeff pushed his not touched plate away and started toward the door.

"Jeff, it's your choice to leave your family, but I found out yesterday Bethany Jameson is my daughter and I will get her back with or without your help."

He turned and looked at me. "What do you mean you found out yesterday?"

I went to talk with Mr. Jameson at the jail,

Bethany was born in Chicago,

And Mr. Jameson admitted to me they was never sure of her real birthday but she was born in 2000 and the mother had been raped, Jeff she is my daughter."

He just stood there looking at me for the longest time and then he started to cry.

My heart melted. "Jeff, sweetie, please come sit down and talk to me."

"Dana if she is your daughter, then she is mine also."

All I could think was Oh thank you Jesus; he is finally feeling how I feel.

I thought he was saying he loves me enough to stay and raise Bethany with me.

But he continued to talk.

"Why couldn't you have just left things as they were? Why did you have to keep digging farer and farer, haven't I been good to you? Haven't I been a good father?"

"Yes Jeff, of course you have." I cried.

Then he became quite, and I just gave him time to collect his thoughts.

"I used to watch you; I thought you were so beautiful, I knew someone like you would never go with someone like me.

I used to fantasize about you, every day and every night you were on my mind.

I would drive by your apartment every morning and follow you to school

Until that one day I got up the nerve to ask you out, it was the happiest day of my life when you said yes.

After we had eaten, I should have left us to fate.

But I couldn't it wasn't enough for me to just let you walk away, I wish I had, I wish with all of my heart I had."

Jeff was scaring me, I stood up, and walked close to the front door all the time not taking my eyes off of him, he didn't seem to notice that I had moved he kept talking, turning my blood cold.

After you drove off that evening from the restaurant I got into my car and I followed you, but then you stopped at that gas station, it was as if everything was working out in my favor.

I went to the parking garage and I waited.

Dana I was sick I had to have you. I had no power over it.

He started to cry again.

"I'm so sorry; but you see that is the reason. I wanted you to forget Bethany because I knew you would find out.

If you would have just listen to me , if you would have just walked away from this child, everything would be fine right now, we could have just went on as a happy family, but you had to have your way, you never wanted that baby remember, that is why you gave her away in the first place.

I picked up my keys and ran out the door by the time I got to my mom's I was shaking uncontrollably.

I sat in the car crying all I could think about was the nightmares I would have over and over, my attacker was the one that was comforting me.

I couldn't go in and let the kids see me so I called mom and told her to send the kids outside to play.

She opened the door for me. “Dana what is wrong?’

“I was crying so hard I couldn’t talk she was trying to calm me down.

“Honey tell me what is wrong, at this time Paul was also trying to calm me.

“It was Jeff; Jeff is the one that assaulted me in that parking garage that night

It was Jeff.”

“What? Dana what are you saying? You aren’t making any sense”

“Mom that is the reason Jeff didn’t want me to find out about Bethany, because

I would find out it was him” I cried, he is her father.”

“Dana, honey you are jumping to conclusions.”

“Mom he is the one that told me, he confessed to it.”

Paul angrily went out the front door.

“Mom stops him” I screamed. She ran after him

"Paul, where are you going?" I heard her calling after him, but it was too late he drove away.

"How could this be happening? He was with me all the time, when I moved out of that apartment, he moved my things

All these years I have been sleeping with the man that I have feared."

"Dana, you have to call the police and tell them, Jeff is a school teacher, he works at a college, and they have to be told." "I know mom you are right I'm never going to get Bethany back now." I cried

Paul came back; he said Jeff wasn't there when he got there.

"What am I going to do? "You and the kids are going to stay here until you are divorced from that madman and then you will get your house.

Honey we are going to make sure you and the kids are okay, we are here with you in this, and you are not alone.

But I say unto you which hear, Love your enemies, do good to them which hate you, Luke 6:2

Chapter Twenty Five

The next few days I walked around like a zombie. Mom and Paul went with me to my house to get our things, after I was sure Jeff was not there.

I talked to my attorney and he advised me to go for adopting Bethany and not bring up the fact that she was the child I had giving away and with Mr. Jameson signing over his parental rights to me, he didn't see a reason I could not adopt her.

I didn't tell him about Jeff, I wasn't telling anyone until I had my daughter home.

I text Jeff and told him I wanted to meet with him right away with my mother and Paul present right outside the door.

"Dana I'm not going to hurt you, I would never hurt you, I love you.

Standing inside the living room I laid down the rules.

"Jeff I have to go to court to get Bethany back and you are going with me,

Because as crazy as it sounds I need us to play the happy family, and I want you to quit your job at the college now, and if you refuse I will go to the police right now, and with a scandal like this, you will never teach again."

"Dana, don't come over here threatening me, because you see it's your word against mine.

How is it going to look on your part, when you married me and had two children with me.

I will help you get your kid back not because of your rules! But because I love you."

"What about your job?" "Well for your information, I have already quit."

"Good, I will be in touch about the dates."

I walked out where Mom and Paul were waiting right outside the door.

After we left there, we went to the Pastor's house to get the kids.

"Dana, are you going to let him go back to school in three weeks to be around those children, he is a rapist."

"No mom, I'm just biding my time for right now to get my daughter back.

And if that can't be done before School starts back, I will tell the authorities what he did to me eight years ago. He will not be around those children I will see to it."

We talked a long time with the pastor and his wife before we went home.

"Mommy where is daddy?' " Daddy is at home sweetie," "When are we going home?" "Katie soon Okay." "Okay", she said.

I had to get prepared for the adoption hearing and I also had to get ready for a new school year for me and for my children.

Andrew would be going to preschool and I had to get him ready for that, plus there was so many things I had to do as a teacher, so I didn't have much time to think about Jeff, I didn't miss him but I prayed every day for God to take away these bad feelings I had towards him help me to forgive him.

I didn't realize how much work went into adopting a child, I moved back into my home, Jeff stayed with a friend until after the adoption was final.

We got to interact with Bethany she was so happy she would get to come live with us.

When the social worker came to our home, her report was that we had a healthy environment and we seemed like a happy family'.

Jeff did everything I had asked him to do and everything went good.

I know now it was God that brought Bethany back into my life.

If it hadn't been for this little girl I would still be living with my rapist.

Jesus said unto him, If thou canst believe, all things are possible to him that believeth. Mark 9:23

Chapter Twenty Six

IT has been a year since I have got my daughter back, and she is adjusting very well, she is making not only good grades in school, she is also making good friends in school and church, Bethany is a very smart little girl, and Katie and Andrew adore her.

Jeff didn't go back to teaching, the last I heard he was living in Kentucky working on a farm of all places.

I did go to the Authorizes.

Not because of what he did to me, but what he might do to someone else.

At first Katie and Andrew asked about their father, but they haven't in a while.

I couldn't understand why he would abandon his children without a word to them, but I didn't know Jeff.

I still loved him and I missed my husband that I thought I was married to, but I didn't miss my attacker.

I still had nightmares sometimes, but I was thankful when I woke up from those nightmares, the man that attacked me was not in my bed anymore.

Bethany is very happy to have a sister and brother, and also grandparents that love her very much.

The other day, I was helping all three children with their church Christmas play about the birth of Jesus. Bethany said "Jesus took my mommy home to heaven, but then he gave me another mommy"

It warmed my heart that she thought of me as her mother, I thought it would take her awhile, but she warmed right up to us and became a part of her family.

I had my house right down the road from my mother and I had my children.

No I didn't have my prince charming.

But two out of three is not bad.

"Grandma's here" Andrew said as Mom walked in the door.

"Hey Mom, what are you up to?"

"I came by to let you know, Paul and I are going to Kentucky , this weekend, Paul's oldest Granddaughter is graduating Sunday, and we will be back Tuesday, and also to let you know we are having a cook out the following Saturday, so don't make any plans."

"Okay what should I bring?" "Whatever you want to bring, we always have more than enough'

Okay where are my hugs?"

She said to the kids that were waiting patiently until she finished talking to me.

My mom treated Bethany as if she has known her from birth, I was glad they had a bond as grandmother and granddaughter.

Bethany loved going to church, she fit right in with every one, it was hard to believe a year ago she was this shy little girl, and as I watch her now running around the church talking to everyone she was my little social butterfly.

My children were the joy of my life.

Tuesday evening when mom got home from her trip, she came over.

The kids were in their rooms doing their homework.

"Dana, I have to tell you something" "What is it mom?"

"Jayson said that he read that Jeff got arrested for assaulting a woman that works on campus a few

towns over from where Jayson lives, the husband was picking her from work and heard her screaming, Jeff was caught red handed

The guy held him down until the police arrived."

I couldn't speak all I could do was cry, cry for the woman and cry for Jeff, for my children.

"We will be praying for Jeff." Mom said as she gave me a hug.

"Thanks Mom, so Will I."

But if ye forgive not men their trespasses, neither will your Father forgive your trespasses Matthew 6:15

Chapter Twenty Seven

It is so funny how your life can change, when I took the teaching position in Chicago I never dreamed my life would go through so many changes

Being attacked, marring my attacker, giving away my baby.

Losing my husband and then getting my baby back, I wondered what was next.

Jeff got twenty years in prison he was also charged with two assaults at the college and that was when he was with me.

My life seemed to be going okay, my children and I are very happy and content, I Started having my dreams again about hearing my baby crying, I didn't understand the dreams.

All I know is that God has seen us through everything and has never left my side.

And I think because of it we all have grown in God.

It has been twenty one years since that move to Chicago and Today

My life has changed so much and I have God and my family to thank.

I know Jeff has a problem and I pray he gets the help he needs, but I'm glad he was in jail because there he won't hurt another woman,

It's sad, his children won't be with their father, and it's sad that Jeff will miss out on his children's lives.

I'm very thankful I have my Mother and also Paul, my family means the world to me.

I know Coy and Sara and also Jaden have spent many hours praying for us

And that is what family does

I am truly blessed and I shouldn't have any complaints.

I'm very proud of myself and my children.

Today I wear that proud smile as I watch my beautiful daughter walk on stage and give her class valedictorian speech.

She was such a beautiful inspiration to our family, she has her own way.

Watching as her and Katie grew up through the years I could see not only in their looks but also in their character how very different they were.

Katie looked just like me, people would offend say, and she loves teaching Sunday School and like me she wants to be a school teacher, she loves being around kids.

Andrew is a very intelligent kid, he looks just like his dad, and he is a dedicated Christian, as all of my children. So why shouldn't I be proud.

"Congratulation Bethany, you were awesome up there, I'm so proud of you."

"Did I? I was so scared I would mess up" "Oh no it was great, I loved your speech." "Thanks Mom"

"Hey Sis, good job, for once I was so proud to be your brother" Andrew, joked with her.

"Funny, she said as she punched him in the arm.

"Where's is Katie?"

"Hanging out with her friends"

"Here she comes" we watched as Katie made her way through the crowd of people

"Yay" she said as she gave her sister a hug. "You were brilliant up there on that stage, did you hear that applause?'

"Thanks Sis."

After all the talking and greeting the teachers and all the pictures, it was time to leave.

"Okay where did your grandparents head off to, we have reservations"

I asked whoever was listening to me.

At the restaurant our table was full of family and friends from school and church

Bethany seemed to have a good time and I was glad, she deserved it.

I was not looking forward to the fall when Bethany would leave for college, she had been accepted in one of the most major and respective colleges around.

The following weekend with the help my church. I gave her a graduation party.

She was the light of the party.

Take delight in the LORD, and he will give you the desires of your heart Psalm 37:4. 4

Chapter Twenty Eight

Mom please don't cry, I will be home at Christmas," "I know I'm sorry I told myself over and over, I was not going to cry."

"Yea mom, it's not like she is leaving forever," Andrew said, trying to make me feel better.

"And just thinks Mom, in a few years, it will be me here at the airport leaving for college." "Thanks a lot Katie was that supposed to make me feel better."

"Come on kids, give your momma a break I remember when she went away to college, it almost killed me" After a tearful goodbye, Bethany was gone and I tried to stay focused on things as not to miss her but it was hard.

A few months later, Katie and Andrew had left for church.

Mom wasn't feeling well so I had decided not to go to church tonight but stay home with her; I was just about to head out the door to go to mom's house when someone knocked on my door.

Answering the door, there stood a young lady who looked very familiar to me.

"May I help you?" "I hope so, she said. "Are you Dana Smith?"

"Yes I am. Do I know you?"

"I have been searching for you for three years; my mom just recently gave me your name. I was born in Chicago Heights on August 15, 200

I don't know the reason but my birth mother put me up for adoption.

Mrs. Smith I think you are my mother.

Made in the USA
Middletown, DE
08 November 2019